FURY DIVINE

LUCAS STONE
BOOK 1

MARK ALLEN

WOLFPACK
PUBLISHING
— EST 2013 —

Fury Divine
Paperback Edition
Copyright © 2023 Mark Allen

Wolfpack Publishing
9850 S. Maryland Parkway, Suite A-5 #323
Las Vegas, Nevada 89183

wolfpackpublishing.com

Paperback ISBN 978-1-63977-966-6
eBook ISBN 978-1-63977-965-9
LCCN 2022951365

FURY DIVINE

PROLOGUE

ASTRIDE HIS FAVORITE GELDING, Lucas Stone spotted the western diamondback rattlesnake a split second before it struck.

"Jaz! Look out!" he yelled, clawing for the .357 Magnum holstered on his hip.

Too late.

The four-foot viper uncoiled in the blink of an eye, triangular head thrust forward by a muscular body, and sank its fangs into the rear fetlock of Jasmine's horse. No rattle, no warning—just the swift, savage strike.

The appaloosa mare bucked frantically at the sharp, sudden injection of venom. Stone watched in helpless horror as his seven-year-old daughter flew from the saddle. Jasmine screamed as she was silhouetted like a rag doll against the hot Texas sun for a single heartbeat.

The scream ended abruptly when she fell to earth, replaced by a sickening crunch as her skull slammed against one of the boulders littering the dusty hillside. Her lifeless body slid down the slope a few feet before coming to a stop, her head twisted at an unnatural angle.

Stone leaped off his horse, gun drawn. His boots

skidded on the rocky soil but he quickly regained his balance, heart hammering in his chest as he whispered, "No, no, no, no..." over and over again, like repeated prayer that could somehow bring about a miracle.

His training helped suppress the panic that tried to seize control, but no amount of training in the world could stop the heart-wrenching fear he felt as he looked at his fallen daughter and faced every parent's worst nightmare.

The diamondback had recoiled after its strike. As he drew a bead with the .357, Stone noticed the snake was missing its rattle. That explained why there had been no warning of the reptile's presence.

The gunshot thundered through the canyon walls and the diamondback's head disappeared in a red mist. The body thrashed and twisted in its death throes as Stone ran past and dropped to his knees next to Jasmine.

He knew instantly his little girl was gone.

Grief hit him like a wrecking ball to the chest.

Tears streaming down his face, he pulled her into his lap and held his daughter until the heartache could no longer be contained. The sorrow welled up from a deep, painful place in his soul and demanded to come out.

Wracked by sobs, his beloved angel cradled in his arms but her spirit no longer there, Stone threw back his head and screamed at the heavens...

ONE

STONE JERKED awake with a broken cry.

As was his way—partly due to natural instinct, partly due to his rigorous training—he came out of sleep with full cognizance. He immediately knew he was in a dark motel room and that his dreams had been haunted by the memory of his daughter's death. Just as they had been haunted for so many nights in the ten years since her passing.

He threw off the covers, letting the cool air of the room get to work evaporating the nightmare sweat beading his skin. If he wanted to really cool down, he could step outside. Winter came early up here in Whisper Falls, New York, a mountain town nestled high in the Adirondack Mountains. It might only be mid-November, but several inches of snow already covered the ground and the night temperatures usually hovered below freezing.

Stone laid there until his body chilled and the tragic memories receded. He then swung his legs over the edge of the bed and stood up, feeling his bare feet press into a carpet that was somewhere between threadbare and sandpaper.

He reached over to the nightstand and touched the Bible sitting there. Not the usual motel Gideon Bible; this was his personal copy. The cover was made of leather, a little beaten and battered, much like himself. It had been in his family for three generations and while there were smaller, thinner, lighter Bibles out there, there were none better. At least not for him. His father had presented it to him when Stone graduated from seminary with a note on the inside cover, written in his father's elegant cursive text, that simply said,

Keep the Faith. ~ Dad

Stone's fingers slid off the Bible and touched the object lying next to the holy book. While the leather had felt warm and soft to the touch, the polished metal of the snub-nosed Colt Cobra .38 Special revolver felt cold and hard. A deadly yin to the Bible's peaceful yang.

Yeah, Stone thought, that's my life. A Bible in one hand, a gun in the other.

His life choices had led to this duality. He had once been a warrior, a man who willingly faced the blood and thunder. The government had trained him, forged him into a lethal weapon, and he had used those skills for the greater good. Or at least what he thought, at the time, was the greater good.

But Jasmine's death changed his outlook. While he had never personally killed a child, they had been there, on the killing fields, the collateral damage of drone strikes or hostage situations or enemy retaliation. Before his daughter's death, the small, broken bodies of the innocents had filled him with a mixture of sadness and rage; after her death, they became nothing but a reminder of his loss, merciless catalysts that resurrected his pain each and every time he saw them.

The so-called greater good came at a cost, and it was a price he was no longer willing to pay.

So he walked away from it all and left his warrior days behind him.

Seeking something else, he turned to his faith, always there but long-buried. He didn't know if he *needed* redemption, but he wanted it.

He decided to become a preacher. He had served the gods of war long enough. Now it was time to just serve God. Wasn't like he had anyone else in his life. His daughter was dead and Theresa, his wife, had left him shortly thereafter. Theresa claimed that seeing him reminded her of Jasmine and she just couldn't live like that. While she claimed that she did not blame him for their daughter's accident, her eyes told a different story.

Stone had let her go. He didn't believe in divorce—he had meant those *'til death do us part* vows—but he also didn't believe in trying to hold on to someone who no longer wanted to be held.

Getting his ministry degree had been a breeze. Finding a church willing to accept him as their pastor had been anything but. His beliefs were rooted in the protestant faith, but he possessed a decidedly liberal—some would call it "worldly"—bent.

That's why he had driven from south Texas to the northern edge of upstate New York. He hoped—prayed —that some small, independent mountain church would be more accepting of his unorthodox ways. Denominations were driven by their rules and Stone was a preacher who hated rules.

He stepped over to the window and cracked the blinds to look outside. A thin layer of snow dusted his red-and-white, '78 Chevy Blazer, one of the few things

Theresa had willingly allowed him to keep in the divorce settlement. Darkness still lingered, dawn just a smudged promise above the mountains that ringed this valley town. The harsh lights of the parking lot gave the snow a jaundiced tinge.

Stone let the blinds fall back in place. He had plenty of time before he needed to be at Faith Bible Church to give his sermon and see if he could convince the congregation he was the right man to fill their preacher vacancy.

He lingered in the shower, cranking up the water temperature to just shy of scalding. The hot spray eased away the aches, pains, and knotted muscles he had accumulated during his three-day road trip from the plains of Texas to the mountains of New York.

Too bad the scars on his body didn't wash away as easily. The bullet wounds and knife marks testified to the grim nature of his former life. A lot of miles, a lot of pain.

After a quick blast of cold water to jolt the last remnants of sleep from his system, Stone toweled off and dressed in a pair of dark blue jeans, white dress shirt, and lightweight hiking boots. He slid into a warm, heavy rancher's coat before picking up a brown-leather, cattle-man-creased cowboy hat with a band made out of diamondback rattlesnake skin. He set the hat on his brown, collar-length hair and pulled it low on his head, putting his honey-colored eyes in shadow.

He slipped the Colt .38 revolver into his coat pocket before picking up the Bible and heading out to find some breakfast.

TWO

THE GIRL FLED and the wolves chased her.

She could hear them hot on her heels as she ran, her bare feet breaking through the frozen crust of snow, the icy crystals shredding her soles.

The wolves were quieter than her, slipping through the thick woods like wraiths. This was their ground and she was the alien, the predators familiar with their surroundings hunting down their lost and helpless prey. Wolves hunting a frightened little lamb.

And she *was* frightened. Had been for a long time, even before she got lost. The sky was dark, the moon masked by swollen clouds that dumped a light but steady snowfall. Snow that filtered down through the skeletal tangle of branches overhead as she plunged through thickets and thorns. Limbs whipped her face, the welts stinging in the cold, night air. She held her hands in front of her as she ran and soon they were torn and tattered as well.

But still she kept running. It was her only chance.

She didn't dare look back. Didn't want to know how much ground the pack had gained. She knew if they caught her, there would be no mercy. The hungry wolves would rip her apart.

She didn't know how long or how far she ran. Her lungs burned, chest heaving. The cold numbed her skin, dulled the pain from the cuts and scratches. Her foot slipped on a patch of ice, and she stumbled into a rock, banging her knee against the unforgiving surface. But still she kept running, a rivulet of blood streaming down her shin for a few seconds before freezing into a red, crusted stripe.

As she glimpsed the shadowy shape of a wolf ghosting in on her flank, she clawed her way over a pile of jumbled logs, the frozen moss crackling beneath her fingertips. She found herself on the edge of a large bog, dead trees and rotten stumps sticking up from the ice like decaying teeth in brackish gums.

She glanced left and spotted a wolf moving in for the kill, teeth bared in a savage snarl. She turned to the right, but a huge boulder blocked her way. She could hear more wolves moving on the other side.

No choice but forward.

Heart hammering as terror churned in her veins, she raced out onto the frozen bog, leaving bloody footprints in the dusting of snow that covered the ice. In front of her, a snowshoe hare burst from cover and fled like a furry rocket. She wished she could run that fast.

But wishes didn't make it so.

Halfway across the frozen swamp, a wolf took her from behind.

A heavy weight crashed into her back and knocked her to the ground. She landed on her belly and skidded across the ice, snow billowing up around her. Her nose smashed off the top of a rock and she heard the crunch as it broke.

She struggled to stand, hands and feet scrabbling on

the snow-slick ice, but the wolf crushed her flat. She screamed, a desperate, terrified cry that echoed through the cold, dead air of the marsh.

The other wolves closed in, circling their prey. She felt dirty paws clawing at her flesh and hot, stinking breath on the back of her neck. Her scream became a sob and then the sob turned into a wet gurgle as sharp pain sliced into her throat. The wolf raised its head and howled at the shrouded moon as blood gushed from her torn jugular.

Her final breath wisped from between her lips and twisted into the air like a vanishing ghost. Her lifeblood melted the snow with its heat before hardening to a crimson glaze on the ice.

Later, the wolves slipped away, their hunger sated, the feast finished.

THREE

WHISPER FALLS WAS a sprawling town situated in a general T-shape formed by the junction of the main street—uncreatively called Main Street—and Wildflower Avenue, with various streets branching off in different directions like potholed capillaries.

Stone had toured the area after he checked into the hotel yesterday afternoon. "Quaint" was really the only way to describe the town. You could feel the character and history of the place as you drove around.

For the most part, Whisper Falls seemed to have resisted the influx of chain stores that often polluted—and eventually crushed—small town living. The motel clerk had proudly mentioned that Wal-Mart had tried to build just up the road and the town board shut them down. The only franchises that Stone could see were McDonalds, Subway, and Dunkin' Donuts. Everything else appeared to be locally-owned mom 'n' pop shops.

The Main Street businesses were as clumped together as any other small town main street in America, all within easy walking distance of one another. But the stores populating Wildflower Avenue were spread further apart. Still walking distance, but you were going to put in some steps.

Spiraling out even further from the center of town were more businesses—garages, delis, diners, accountants—which leant proof that Whisper Falls might only boast a population of 3,000, but it was a thriving little community.

Stone had only been in town about sixteen hours, but he already liked it here. Now he just needed to convince Faith Bible Church to give him a reason to stay.

Main Street was mostly dark as he drove through town. Clearly Whisper Falls was not the kind of place that sprang to life at the crack of dawn, at least not on Sunday mornings.

He headed out just past the town limits to the Birch Bark Diner, a roadside eatery he had spotted the day before. As he steered the Chevy Blazer into the parking lot, he saw the place was lit up and open for business.

When he stepped inside, a bell above the door jangled to announce his arrival. Two elderly men sitting at the counter—the kind of men who looked like they had been coming to the Birch Bark religiously for the last forty years to have their morning cup of coffee—turned and gave him the once-over. Their faces were neither friendly nor hostile, just matter-of-fact as they examined the stranger in their midst.

"Morning," Stone said, removing his hat as he stood by a brass sign with black lettering that ordered him to Wait To Be Seated.

"Morning," the old man on the left replied, while the one on the right just nodded. They both studied him, eyes bright and piercing beneath bushy white brows. Then, with the kind of synchronicity that a cheerleading team would have killed for, they both turned back to their coffee. Amused, Stone wondered if he had just passed or failed some kind of small-town test.

A woman emerged from the back, a plate of steaming food in each hand, the door automatically swinging shut behind her. She looked to be somewhere in her mid- to late-30s, her brunette hair pulled back in a short ponytail to reveal a pretty face. She wore black jeans and a white polo shirt with the words Birch Bark Diner embroidered on the left side and H. Bennett on the other. A large silver cross hung from a chain around her neck.

Spotting Stone standing there, she called out, "You can ignore that sign and seat yourself, stranger." She tossed him a smile. "As you can see, we're not exactly hopping yet." She moved behind the bar to serve the pair of old timers their plates of scrambled eggs, hash, and home fries.

"Thanks." As Stone headed for a nearby table, he saw another patron sitting alone in the corner booth, a newspaper spread out in front of him, an empty plate pushed to the side. He had a mug of coffee—well, Stone assumed it was coffee; could be tea or cocoa, he supposed—raised to his lips and his eyes studied Stone over the rim as he sipped.

Stone returned the frank, appraising stare and then gave a short nod of greeting before shucking off his coat and draping it over the back of a chair. He didn't much care for the vibes coming off the man in the corner booth. But he had come here for breakfast, not trouble. He set his hat down on the empty chair to his right before picking up the laminated menu lying on the table next to the napkin dispenser.

The waitress strolled over with a pot of coffee in her hand as he scanned the selections. "Morning, stranger," she greeted, and poured him a cup of coffee without asking.

"Morning." Stone watched the black, steaming-hot liquid fill the mug. "How'd you know I wanted coffee?"

"This is mountain country," she replied. "Up here, everyone drinks coffee and if you don't, people don't trust you. Since you're a stranger to these parts, figured I would just go ahead and help you out." Her smile was warm and honest. "You don't want folks around here taking a disliking to you right off the bat. It'll take you twenty years to get back in their good graces."

"So this is a very important cup of coffee."

"Your reputation depends on it, stranger."

"Stone."

"Come again?"

"That's my name," he replied. "Lucas Stone. Now you can stop calling me stranger."

"Lucas, huh? You stuck on that, or is Luke okay?"

"I prefer Luke, actually. Lucas sounds so pretentious, know what I mean?"

She laughed lightly. "Well, we can't have any pretentiousness around here. I'm Holly, by the way."

"Nice to meet you."

"Bet you say that to all the girls." Her eyes twinkled mischievously. "You sticking around town or just passing through?"

"You got a preference?"

"No comment," she replied with a smile. "But speaking of preferences, you see something you like?"

Stone grinned.

Holly rolled her eyes good-naturedly. "On the menu, I mean."

"Let's keep it simple. Couple eggs, over-easy, with some bacon and home fries."

"A plain breakfast for a plain man." Holly smirked as she jotted down his order.

"Ouch." Stone feigned pain. "That hurts."

Holly winked. "The truth usually does, Luke." She turned and headed for the kitchen to put in his ticket.

There was no extra sway in her hips—or anything sensual for that matter—but Stone found himself admiring her figure as she walked away. Not in a lustful way or anything like that. He didn't strip her with his eyes or imagine getting horizontal with her. No, she was just a good-looking woman and he appreciated God's handiwork.

Stone glanced over at the man in the corner booth and caught his eyes glued to Holly's backside like it was a firm, heart-shaped magnet and his pupils were made out of metal. He looked like a love-struck puppy dog.

The man looked up, met Stone's gaze, and realized he'd been busted. His face turned red, then he gathered up his coat, slid from the booth, and approached Stone's table. Gesturing toward the empty chair across from Stone, he asked, "Mind if I sit, sir?"

"Long as you don't call me 'sir.' The name's Stone. Luke, if you're more comfortable with first names."

The man sat down. He looked to be in his mid-50s, with a thick, black, gray-flecked mane of hair that crowned a stern face. "Oh, I know who you are, Mr. Stone."

Stone was instantly wary. He had made a lot of enemies during his gunslinger days. But the man's hands were in sight, so there wasn't a gun pointed at him underneath the table. "You do?"

The man nodded.

"Guess that means you've got me at a disadvantage," Stone said.

"I'm David White."

Stone relaxed. White was the head deacon at Faith Bible Church and his designated point of contact. Pretty safe to say that White wasn't going to try to kill him. Not right here in the diner anyway, before he'd even eaten his breakfast. Maybe after he gave his sermon.

Stone stuck out his hand. "After all the emails and phone calls, it's good to finally meet you in person, David."

The head deacon made no move to shake his hand. "Mr. White."

Stone kept his hand hanging out there well beyond the point of awkwardness, then let it drop. "Sorry?"

"Please call me Mr. White or Deacon White. Or just simply White, if you absolutely must. Only my friends call me David and you and I are not yet friends." He sighed. "And to be frank with you, Mr. Stone, I doubt we ever will be."

"Some people might consider that rude."

"I'm not trying to be rude," White said. "I'm trying to be honest."

"That's very Christ-like of you."

White either didn't catch the sarcasm or chose to ignore it. "Do you want to know why I'm being honest like this? Do you want to know why I don't think we can be friends?"

"Don't really care," Stone said. "But I'm guessing you're going to tell me anyway."

"That's right, I am," White replied. "Because I think you have a right to know. You see, Mr. Stone, it's like this —Faith Bible Church is *my* church."

Stone opened two sugar packets and dumped them into his coffee. "Last time I checked, the church belongs to God. Or, for that matter, if you want to get right down to where the rubber meets the road, the church is the people. Nobody owns it."

"You know what I mean," White said.

Stone picked up the spoon and stirred his coffee, clanking the silverware off the side of the mug. "Actually,

David—" Yeah, he was just being petty now, but he would ask for forgiveness later—"I don't think I do."

"Let's boil it down to brass tacks and cut to the chase, shall we?" White said. "Every church has that certain someone who runs the place behind the scenes, the one who makes the calls and pull the strings. Sometimes it's the pastor, but sometimes it's not." He paused, seemingly for dramatic effect. "At Faith Bible Church, that person is me."

"So you fancy yourself the power behind the pulpit, that what you're telling me?"

"I don't *fancy*," White replied. "I *am*."

Stone took a sip of his coffee. "Good to know."

White looked perplexed. "That's all you're going to say?"

"Was I supposed to say something else?"

"I assumed you would want to put forth your position."

Stone set down his coffee and looked at his watch. "I'll put forth my position about ninety minutes from now, when I'm standing behind the pulpit...of *God's* church."

White's face reddened. He pushed back his chair and stood up. "Trust me, Mr. Stone, you won't be in this town long. I've watched your sermons online and read quite a bit of your published work and I'm telling you that my church—and this whole town, for that matter—doesn't need your kind of cowboy Christianity."

Stone smiled at him but there was steel behind his eyes. "Guess we'll find out soon enough, won't we?"

White glanced over at the counter where Holly refilled the old men's coffee cups and pretended to not be eavesdropping on his and Stone's conversation. His eyes slid back to Stone as he leaned in close to hide his next words from Holly's ears. "Also, just so we're clear, Mr.

Stone, I see the way you're looking at the prettiest wait-ress in Garrison County. Do yourself a favor and get those kind of trashy thoughts out of your head."

"It's not like that," Stone said.

"It *is* like that." White practically hissed the words. "But it needs to stop. Holly is mine. You understand? I'm going to marry that woman someday."

Stone lowered his voice. "Does Holly know that?"

White's face crumpled. "Well, no…"

"Then what makes you so sure?"

The head deacon's face tightened again. "God told me."

Stone leaned back in his chair. "Then it sounds like you've got nothing to worry about." He frowned with exaggerated seriousness. "Unless, of course, you don't have faith."

White looked offended. "I have all the faith I need."

"Glad to hear it. So we're done here?" Stone phrased it as a question but hardened his tone to make it clear it was more of a *get-the-hell-away-from-me* command.

White took the hint. "See you at church," he said. The bell above the door tinkled as he exited the diner, a cold burst of air rushing in before the door closed behind him.

Holly showed up at Stone's table a minute later with a plate of hot food. "Here you go, Luke." As she topped off his coffee, she said, "I see you had the pleasure of meeting Deacon White."

"He missed his calling. Warm and friendly as he is, he should've been a Wal-Mart greeter."

Holly chuckled. "He's a bit of a jerk sometimes, and when he's not being a jerk, he's busy being a sanctimo-nious prick." She quickly slapped a hand over her mouth. "Sorry about the language. I overheard you're a preacher."

"No need to apologize. A little cursing never killed anyone."

She tilted her head as if studying him in a new light. "You're telling me you're a preacher but you aren't bothered by four letter words?"

He gave her a wink. "Hell, no."

She laughed and headed back toward the kitchen, saying over her shoulder, "Enjoy your breakfast." As he bit into a slab of bacon just slightly smaller than a barn board, he heard her mutter under her breath, "A preacher who swears. I'll be damned."

Smiling inwardly, Stone thought, *Not if I can help it.*

Hunger kicked in and he tore through his breakfast like a man on a mission. The coffee was hot, the eggs perfectly cooked, the bacon crisp, and the home fries just the way he liked them—no onions. If there were onions in Heaven, he'd rather go to Hell, preacher or not.

Holly cleared his plate, refilled his coffee, and he took his time savoring it since he had some time to kill before heading over to the church. Finally, he tossed some money on the table, including a generous tip, then stood up, pulled on his coat, and settled his hat on his head.

Holly came over with an amused look on her face. "Don't see too many cowboy hats 'round these parts," she said, adopting an exaggerated Texan drawl.

"Maybe I'll be a trendsetter."

She pointed at the hatband. "What's up with the snakeskin?"

Stone rarely told anyone the truth about that, especially people he had just met. Instead, he made up stories. "Went camping back in Texas and woke up one morning to find this rattler curled up next to me in my sleeping bag. Killed him with my bare hands and figured he'd make a real nice band for my hat."

Holly cocked her head. "You're kidding me, right?"

"Which part?"

"All of it."

Stone grinned. "No, I really did go camping in Texas."

As he headed for the door, Holly laughed and called out, "Good luck, Luke." With a wink, she added, "Give 'em hell."

"Pretty sure my job is to give them Heaven," Stone replied. "But maybe a little hell will come along for the ride."

He closed the door behind him and stepped out into the cold November morning. The sun had crested the mountains, spilling golden light down the slopes laden with snow-topped pines and white-barked birches. He breathed deep, relishing the feel of the icy air cooling his throat while the clean mountain scent reminded him of home. It smelled woodsier than Texas, which featured more of a grassy, prairie scent, but the sensation was similar. They both smelled like rustic, wide-open spaces, just the way he liked it.

Yeah, I could get used to it here.

He climbed into the Chevy Blazer and headed back toward Whisper Falls where the church sat on the western edge of town.

Time to preach his guts out and see if they'd let him stay.

FOUR

FAITH BIBLE CHURCH was your standard, white, box-like building with a steeple stabbing up into the sky and stained-glass windows adding a touch of color. Nothing fancy, but it had character.

You could tell the church had been there a long time. As he paused in the parking lot to gaze up at the simple cross that adorned the top of the steeple, Stone felt the history emanating from the place. It was the kind of homespun heritage that the million dollar megachurches would never be able to replicate.

A place of simple people with simple faith and that was not a criticism or condemnation. Far as Stone was concerned, people piled way too much other crap onto the straight-forward message that Jesus taught during his thirty-three years on earth.

Inside the church, Stone sat in the front pew and surveyed his surroundings. The clouds that had brought the early morning snow showers had quickly vanished when the sun came up and the light had a cold, brittle edge as it speared through the stained glass.

The sanctuary was small, but the vaulted ceiling gave

it a more spacious feel than the square footage suggested. Dark wood paneled the walls, which were adorned with paintings of various Bible scenes, including Noah's Ark, David and Goliath, and of course, the crucifixion. The latter featured no blood, most likely to avoid traumatizing the younger children scattered through the congregation.

Large ceiling fans dangled from the exposed, rustic, rough-hewn rafters but the blades were still. No need for cooling down this late in the year, but Stone wondered if they would get the job done in August. Even up here in the Adirondacks, the temperatures could climb well into the 80s and sometimes even the 90s. He saw no sign of central air conditioning and seriously doubted the church could afford it. If he got the job, maybe he would use his own funds to have it installed, along with some other improvements and renovations. He had socked away plenty of money during his warrior days. Spending some of it on this little church seemed like a righteous use of the cash.

Blood money used as a blessing, damn straight.

Deacon White stood behind the pulpit, leading the worship portion of the service. His voice was surprisingly rich and powerful. The worship band consisted of a keyboardist, guitarist, and drummer, and they played a hodgepodge mix of classic hymns and contemporary Christian music tunes. On the wall behind them hung a large wooden cross.

Stone had learned that in the absence of a pastor, White had been handling preaching duties and the general oversight of the church. He wondered if that's where some of the man's acrimony came from. Maybe White felt like *he* should be the pastor of Faith Bible Church, not some outsider.

When the last song had been sung—a rousing rendition of *The Old Rugged Cross*—White took prayer requests. One elderly woman—a widow named Natasha Unser, he later learned—asked him to pray that the coy-wolves would stop killing her farm animals. Then an older couple asked for prayer for their granddaughter, who had been missing for nearly a week. Fighting back tears, they said Sheriff Camden had no leads and now God was their only hope.

"God is *always* our only hope," Deacon White said, and Stone couldn't quite tell if it was meant to be admonishment or encouragement. Before he could figure it out, the head deacon led everyone in a short prayer and then introduced Stone.

But before he relinquished the pulpit, White took a cheap shot.

"I had the opportunity to meet with Mr. Stone earlier this morning and, well, I must be honest, folks, I just don't think he's the right fit for our humble little church. But everyone deserves a chance, right? So let's hear Mr. Stone preach the Word and we'll hold the vote following this evening's service."

He stepped down from the pulpit with a smug smile and gestured for Stone to take his place. As the two men passed, White snidely whispered, "Good luck."

Stone managed to keep his mouth shut, but the two-word response he mentally fired back at the sabotaging deacon wouldn't be found in any Bible.

Behind the pulpit, Stone faced the congregation, feeling like he'd been hamstrung before he even got a chance to start. He'd prepared a generic sermon, planning on playing it safe. But as he looked out at the faces watching him, many of them already frowning, he realized it would take something bolder to overcome Deacon White's influence.

So he decided to tell them the truth.

"Brothers and sisters," he said, not even trying to tone down his Texas accent, "Deacon White could very well be right. I might not be a good fit for this church. All depends on what you're looking for in a pastor."

"Someone who loves the Lord!" a man in the back row called out and several members of the congregation nodded in agreement.

Stone nodded as well. "Sure, I get that, and I promise you that I do. I took a vow to serve God." He gripped the sides of the pulpit and leaned forward, face serious. "But I did *not* take a vow to serve a bunch of legalistic, manmade rules. God made it clear in the Bible that He looks on the heart. Far as I'm concerned, it's what's in your heart that matters, not whether or not you check all the boxes on some 'What It Takes to Be a Good Christian' list."

From the front row, Deacon White, face reddened with self-righteous rage, snarled, "The Bible has rules to follow. Any *real* Christian knows that."

"The Bible isn't about rules," Stone countered. "The Bible is about a relationship. A relationship between God and man." He leaned back from the pulpit and straightened his shoulders. "Look, when it comes to preaching—and faith in general—I like to keep it raw and real. I don't care if you believe in creation or evolution. I don't think it matters if you have a beer or if you abstain. I think God hates the gossip that rolls off our tongues way more than He cares about four-letter words." He tapped his chest, just left of center, right in the place he had put many a bullet in many a man. "What's in here is what matters."

Several heads in the crowd nodded in agreement. Which meant that not everyone in this church was a Deacon White type. He at least had a chance and that's all a man could ask for.

"I come from Texas, in case you couldn't tell from my accent," Stone continued, eliciting some chuckles from the congregation. "Out there, it's God and guns country, where we believe in living a good life, keeping your word, and doing what's right even when it's hard. I can tell up here in the North Country, it's the same way." His eyes scanned the people seated in the pews, doing his best to meet each and every gaze. "So please believe me when I say that I know what kind of men and women you are, and I'll do my damnedest to be the kind of preacher you deserve."

Deacon White looked like he was about to have a coronary from hearing a swear word spoken from the pulpit.

"Thanks for your time," Stone finished, "and God bless."

He stepped down to let White close the service. As the two men passed, the head deacon hissed, "You're finished here, Stone."

"Guess we'll just have to see which way God rolls the dice," Stone replied.

———

That evening, Stone drove to the picturesque village of Lake Placid and enjoyed dinner at a Tex-Mex restaurant called Desperados. The bartender informed him their margaritas were to die for, but he stuck with his usual drink—Jack and Coke, lots of ice, easy on the Jack. It paired well with a plate of nachos and a pair of chicken chimichangas that could have given the best in Texas a run for its money.

Afterwards, he strolled down the main street of the village, an eclectic mix of retail outlets, quaint shops, hotels, bars, and restaurants. His cowboy hat drew a couple of odd glances, but for the most part the people he passed on the sidewalk were friendly enough.

When he got tired of playing tourist, he drove back to his hotel room in Whisper Falls and waited. The call came shortly after 9:00 p.m.

Faith Bible Church had decided to make him their new pastor. The vote had been unanimous save for one.

Stone wasn't one to gloat, but he couldn't help but smile when he thought about just how pissed Deacon White must be right about now.

FIVE

STONE LAY prone behind the rifle and tried to ignore the fact that he felt right in his element with a gunstock against his shoulder, his eye to a scope, and his finger curled around a trigger.

He was nestled in the brush and bramble at the base of a grain silo perched on a small rise that overlooked a large pasture. He wore white-patterned camo to help him blend into the snow and hide his presence from the wary eyes of the predators he hunted.

Stone had spent the last two weeks going around town and introducing himself. He had fallen into a daily ritual of breakfast at the Birch Bark where his food came with a welcome side order of warm, witty conversation from Holly. After that, it was back to the church for a few hours of sermon preparation, followed by a quick lunch, and then he spent the afternoon visiting his congregation.

By the time he made it out to Natasha Unser's farm yesterday and told her that if she needed anything, don't hesitate to ask, the feisty old widow had wasted no time.

"Need somebody to shoot the damn coy-wolves running around here," she had said. "First they killed my cats, then they got my dog, and now they've started picking off my livestock. Just last week the fleabags took down a baby goat. Can't let anything out of the barn for long because if I do, those sons of bitches will drag them down. My husband Amos, God rest his soul, used to take care of any shooting that needed to be done around here, but he's been gone going on six years now."

"I know my way around a rifle," Stone had said, thinking that was one hell of an understatement. "I'd be happy to come over and pop a couple coy-wolves for you."

"I'd appreciate that, Pastor Luke. I'll see you tomorrow morning."

Tucked in the shadow of the silo, Stone grinned at the memory. He hadn't actually said when he'd come back and do some coy-wolf hunting, but Natasha Unser had made it perfectly clear when she expected him. He had originally planned on skipping breakfast this morning and hiking up Whisper Mountain to see the waterfall from which the town derived its name. He wanted to make it up there before the drifts deepened and closed the trail until spring. But helping out the elderly widow definitely took priority.

Back when he had hunted human enemies, Stone had meticulously researched his targets before ever settling the crosshairs on their heads or chests. The predators he currently pursued might walk on four legs rather than two, but Stone had still done his homework.

He had spent over two hours the previous night reading articles on the coy-wolves of the Adirondack Mountains and quickly realized there was little consensus among the experts. But from what he pieced together, it appeared these northeastern coy-wolves were a four-in-one hybrid of coyotes, eastern wolves, western gray wolves, and dogs. They were larger than coyotes but not quite as large as a pureblooded wolf. They worked more cooperatively in packs than coyotes and tended to be more aggressive as well.

Which is why he now lay prostrate in a bunch of brambles, the butt of the Remington 700 SPS Varmint rifle tucked against his shoulder. Chambered in .308, the gun was more than capable of reaching out long distances and blasting a big hole right through a coy-wolf's boiler room. The predator would be blown right off its feet before it even knew what hit it.

Optics were provided by a Bushnell 3-9x50mm scope with a Multi-X reticle. He cranked up the scope to maximum magnification since it was over two hundred yards to the fence line on the far side of the pasture, where he had hidden an electronic wounded-rabbit call. He figured if the coy-wolves were willing to chow down on housecats, they would be tempted by a screaming hare. He could activate the call with the remote lying on the ground beside him.

Since the barn and silo sat on a small rise, his position was elevated above the pasture, meaning any shot would be at a slight downward angle. The pasture itself was flat —Natasha had explained that sometimes she planted potatoes in it, other times she just used it for grazing— and covered with several inches of snow. Stalks of winter wheat poked up through the surface here and there.

The pasture ended at the bottom of a sloped ridge, a wooden-post-and-barbed-wire fence-line marking the point where the flatland stopped. Pines covered the ridge, forming tight clusters with open spaces between them. Scanning the terrain through the scope, Stone saw that thin saplings grew in those bare spots. When the leaves were on the trees, the entire ridge would be cloaked, the barren spaces of the winter months filled in by the foliage of spring, summer, and early fall.

Stone glanced over his shoulder, scanning beyond the partially-frozen wetlands on the other side of the road to the mountains looming in the distance. The sun had crested the high peaks, blessing the valley with warming rays, and Stone could feel the cold morning air start to climb a couple of degrees.

Time to hunt.

He picked up the remote and activated the call. Seconds later, the shrill, piercing scream of a dying rabbit cut through the silence of the morning. He imagined the sound floating up the ridge, into the nooks and crannies that formed the woodlands, and hopefully reaching the ears of the coy-wolves.

Despite their aggression, Stone knew the predators would be cautious. He had some time to kill—no pun intended—before they would appear, and that was assuming they were even in the vicinity right now and within earshot of the rabbit screams.

Being behind a rifle again resurrected memories of so many other times he had laid in wait for a target to enter the kill-zone. Missions so covert they would never be declassified. Operations so dark that regular black ops seemed little more than pale gray by comparison. He had done things he could never talk about with anyone, things he didn't *want* to talk about with anyone. Hell, he sometimes even had trouble talking to *God* about them.

Did those things need to be done? Yes. Because sometimes the only way to deal with evil is to slay it. But no matter how righteous the killing, it came at a steep cost. He suffered no regrets at having walked away from it all.

His naked eye caught movement up on the ridge. Something moved slow and furtive, creeping out from beneath some ground-level pine boughs.

Stone pivoted the rifle until the creature filled the scope, then smiled at the intense look on the bobcat's face as it crept closer to where it believed a dying rabbit was ready for the taking. *Sorry, little fella, but you're going to be very disappointed.*

He kept his eye glued to the scope as the wild feline picked its way down the slope, tufted ears pricked up, eyes fixed on the base of the old fence post where Stone had hidden the electronic call. The rabbit shrieks rang out at regular intervals, drawing the cat in ever closer.

Then, as if lightning had struck its stubby tail, the bobcat spun around and bolted toward the far end of the pasture as fast as its paws could carry it away.

For a second, Stone assumed the cat had just spooked because it couldn't see any wounded rabbit where its ears had identified one should be. But when he pulled his eyes back from the scope, he spotted the real reason for the bobcat's flight.

Three coy-wolves sprinted down the fence line, zeroing in on where they believed the rabbit to be. Distracted by the bobcat, Stone had missed their silent approach.

He reacted quickly to compensate for his error. He was no stranger to shooting fast.

He got the lead coy-wolf in his crosshairs. For just half a second, he admired the primal beauty of the beast as it ran, kicking up snow, thick fur coat ruffling in the wind. Then he slid the crosshairs forward, leading the predator, and pulled the trigger.

The Remington recoiled against his shoulder. The sound of the shot cracked the morning sky like thunder. The bullet struck home and the coy-wolf went down in a tumbling heap that sent white powder flying in all directions. The dead predator skidded to a stop against a fence post, causing the rusted barbed wire to shiver in the cold sunlight.

Stone worked the bolt with the fluid speed of someone who had performed the action thousands of times. The spent cartridge arced to the ground as he jacked the bolt forward to load another round into the chamber.

The remaining two coy-wolves spun in their tracks the second the first shot rang out. They fled back the way they came, tucked low to the ground, racing along the fence line like greyhounds streaking toward the finish line.

Stone got the scope on the next one. Even at this distance, a moving target was well within his sniping capabilities. Once, during an operation in Afghanistan, he'd picked off a Taliban machine-gunner on the back of a pickup truck doing at least forty-five miles per hour across a dry riverbed from nearly 500 meters out. Nailing a running coy-wolf at two hundred yards was a piece of cake.

He smoothly stroked the trigger, riding out the rifle's kick, and the second coy-wolf went down thrashing in the blood-spattered snow.

The last coy-wolf switched evasive tactics. It veered left, slipped between the stands of barbed wire, and ran up the ridge. As Stone cycled the bolt-action, the predator darted into a thick cluster of pine trees and vanished.

Stone waited a full minute, watching through the scope in case the coy-wolf reappeared in one of the open spaces. But after sixty seconds, it became clear that the predator had either fled the area or was hunkered down under cover. If the latter was the case, it might not move for hours. Stone considered tracking it, but decided not to bother. Two dead coy-wolves was a solid morning's work.

He stood up and stretched, loosening muscles grown stiff from the cold. He used the remote to silence the electronic call, retrieved his spent brass, canted the rifle over his shoulder, and struck out across the pasture.

The snow crunched under his boots as he walked. He inhaled deeply, enjoying the cool sensation of the fresh mountain air. The pungent scent of the nearby pines masked the earthy smells of the barnyard.

A slight breeze ruffled the dead coy-wolves' fur coats, giving them the illusion of life. But closer inspection revealed the blood-stained snow, glazed eyes, and lolling tongues that signified death. Neither predator had suffered unnecessarily; both bullets scored clean kills.

He dragged the carcasses to the top of the ridge and dropped them into the gully on the other side, fresh meat for the forest scavengers. Regular coyotes would slink in later tonight under cover of darkness and start stripping the bodies down to the bones. Even the other coy-wolves might come around and feast on their own fallen pack members.

He walked back to the farmhouse, said goodbye to Natasha Unser, who thanked him profusely, and then climbed into the Blazer. As he cranked the heater and waited for the engine to warm up, he smiled to himself. The day was off to a good start. He even had time to hit the Birch Bark for breakfast. The thought of seeing Holly made him warm before the heater even started to blow hot air.

Yeah, he told himself, *it's gonna be a good day.*

Then his cell phone rang and it all went straight to hell.

SIX

STONE ANSWERED on the third ring. "This is Stone."

A baritone voice on the other end said, "Pastor Stone, this is Sheriff Camden."

Stone had only met the sheriff briefly, when the lawman stopped by his house one evening to introduce himself. He had picked up from people in town that Grant Camden was a fixture in Garrison County, having been elected sheriff for the last twenty years. Most folks seemed to consider him lazy or, at best, "marginally competent." But he kept getting elected because nobody bothered to run against him.

"Morning, sheriff," Stone replied. "What can I do for you?"

"You know the Wadfords?"

"Sure, they're members of the church."

"So you're aware their twelve-year-old grand-daughter has been missing for the last three weeks?"

"Yeah, I know. Her name's Sadie." He didn't mention that the Wadfords felt the sheriff had done the absolute bare minimum to find her. "We've been praying for her."

"Well, you can stop praying," Camden said. "She's been found."

"Thank God."

"Sure, if you want to thank God for a dead kid, go right ahead."

Stone felt a cold, hard fist clutch his heart. "She's dead?"

"Trapper found her body—or at least what's left of it —over in Sinkhole Hollow Swamp. Know where that is?"

"Yes."

"Thought you might want to be here when the Wadfords show up. They'll need a shoulder to cry on. Figured that's your line of work."

"Why are they coming out to the swamp?"

Sheriff Camden let out a frustrated sigh. "Because my dumbass deputy fucked up and called them, that's why." He didn't apologize for his language. "They've got about a thirty minute drive from Tupper Lake. Be good if you could get here before they do."

"Be there in fifteen."

"Thanks. See you then." Camden hung up.

Stone backed the Blazer out onto the road and hit the gas. Sinkhole Hollow Swamp was about twelve miles to the northeast, in the wild country beyond the borders of Whisper Falls.

He ducked down some side roads to avoid the center of town, passing the Birch Bark along the way. He regretted missing his morning chat with Holly, but right now there were more pressing things to take care of.

Anthony Wadford and his wife Betty had raised Sadie since she was three years old, after her parents were killed by a drunk logging truck driver. They loved and adored her like their own daughter. Her death would devastate them.

Stone drove with a troubled spirit. His silent prayers

were stripped down to their naked essence, full of raw, bare-boned emotion.

Damn it, Lord, why do you let children suffer?

It was one of the hardest questions for a man of faith to answer.

Because there was no answer.

Stone didn't know what he was going to say when the Wadfords looked at him with tear-stained eyes and asked him why God let their little girl die.

———

The flashing lights of the emergency vehicles kaleidoscoped the morning air with pulses of red and blue as Stone pulled his Blazer over to the side of the dirt road. He climbed out of the truck and pulled his hat low. The wind had picked up a bit and he flipped up the collar of his rancher's coat to keep the chill at bay.

As he approached, he spotted a miserable-looking man sitting on a fallen cedar log, hands shaking. The guy wore a knit cap, heavy jacket, jeans so thick they had to be insulated, and knee-high rubber boots. His stubbled cheeks glowed red in the cold and half-frozen snot drizzled down into his patchy mustache.

A group of men surrounded the man, including Sheriff Camden. He broke away as Stone approached, walking over to greet him. He wore a black bomber jacket with a badge pinned on the left side.

"Thanks for coming so quick, Pastor Stone." The sheriff extended his hand.

"Just call me Luke," Stone said, shaking hands. "Or Stone, if you prefer."

"Stone'll work, if that suits you better."

"It does." Stone nodded toward the man on the log. "That the trapper that found Sadie?"

Camden glanced over at the guy. "Yeah, that's him. Found her about a half-mile back. I've got a couple of my boys bringing her out." He shook his head. "Ain't got a clue what she was doing back there. This swamp is some bad country."

"Any idea what happened to her?"

"The damn coy-wolves, would be my guess. She's all tore up and their tracks are all around the body."

"Didn't know they would attack humans," Stone said.

"They don't normally," Camden replied. "And I seriously doubt they would go after a full-grown man, or even a woman. But a little girl like Sadie? Catch her out here in the swamp and yeah, they'd take her down."

Now Stone regretted not being able to nail the third coy-wolf earlier over at the Unser farm. Sounded like they needed to be put down. Maybe in between his pastoral duties, he would put in some time predator hunting.

"Under the circumstances," the sheriff continued, "I'm sure the coroner will order an autopsy, but I think it's pretty clear Sadie got lost in the woods and got herself killed. Happens at least a couple times a year up here in the High Peaks."

"Still doesn't explain what she was doing out here," Stone said.

Camden shrugged. "I'm guessing we'll never know the answer to that."

Right, because actually conducting an investigation is too much work for you. Stone bit down on the harsh words, keeping the thought to himself.

Motion in the swamp drew his attention. Two men wearing jackets similar to Camden's—his deputies, no doubt—weaved along a narrow game trail, carrying a body bag between them as they navigated the frozen terrain.

"Excuse me," the sheriff said, "but I need to get back to work. Thanks again for coming, Stone. The Wadfords should be here soon. I'm leaving it up to you to take care of them."

It sounded like an order to Stone, which he found irritating, but he let it go. "I'll do my best, Sheriff."

Camden nodded, then rejoined the group of men as the deputies emerged from the swamp with the body.

Stone edged closer as the deputies—he recognized Cade Valentine, the rookie on the force, but hadn't met the others—carefully set Sadie's bagged corpse down on the ground, the snow hard-packed from so many feet trampling the area.

Sheriff Camden knelt down next to the dead girl as a man—Stone would later learn he was the Garrison County coroner—leaned over and unzipped the body bag to inspect the corpse.

One of the deputies turned away and vomited all over a nearby stump.

The sheriff glanced at him with a disgusted look and snapped, "Get ahold of yourself, man."

"Sorry, Sheriff," the deputy said, but he avoided looking at the corpse again.

In his former life, Stone had witnessed death a thousand different ways. He had become desensitized to the horrible trauma that could be inflicted on the human anatomy. So glimpsing the savage wounds that mangled Sadie's young body—it looked like the coy-wolves had ripped her throat out right down to the spine—didn't bother him from that standpoint.

What *did* bother him were the heartbreaking memories dredged up by seeing her body. Even though Sadie was older than Jasmine had been, seeing her lying there, cold and broken, reminded him of his dead daughter. They were the kind of memories that haunted a father forever. The loss of a child left a scar that never healed, a hurt that never truly went away.

Stone turned and walked back to his truck, tears stinging his eyes. He felt no shame at crying—hell, even Jesus wept—but he preferred to shed his tears in private, away from the watching eyes of others.

By the time the Wadfords arrived at the scene, he had regained his composure. He switched from grieving father mode to comforting shepherd mode as Anthony and Betty, their faces stricken with grief, tried to run over to where Sadie was being loaded into the back of the coroner's wagon. Stone held them back, holding one with each arm, as they both sobbed, leaning against him for support.

He knew exactly how they felt, the horror poisoning the very depths of their souls, the overwhelming loss that felt too painful to be true, like some dark nightmare from which they begged God to wake them up.

Stone held them tight and spoke words of comfort, sharing their heartache, offering them sincerity rather than clichés and platitudes. What he did not tell them was the cold, hard truth.

Their lives would never be the same.

SEVEN

THE NEXT MORNING, Stone grabbed his usual table at the Birch Bark. Not the one he sat at during his first visit, when Deacon White had so warmly welcomed him to the neighborhood. Since then, he had switched to the corner table that put his back to the wall and his face to the door. He might not be a gunslinger anymore, but old habits died hard.

He hadn't slept much the night before. He had spent most of the day guiding the Wadfords through their emotional devastation and most of the night staring at his bedroom ceiling, wondering if his prayers were getting any further than the crack in the sheetrock. He tossed and turned as he pondered the enigmatic ways of God and why He allowed suffering to hold so much sway over His creation.

Now he felt not just physically exhausted, but spiritually as well. Not a great combination.

Good thing Holly was here to cheer him up.

"You look like crap," she announced as she poured him a much-needed cup of coffee.

"Thanks," he said. "You really know how to make a guy feel better."

She sat down in the chair across from him. "Rough night?"

"Preacher or not, sometimes the questions keep you awake."

"What kind of questions?"

"The kind that don't have easy answers."

Her bright blue eyes searched his face. "This about Sadie Wadford?"

"Yeah." He took a large swig of coffee, hoping the caffeine would kick in quick. "Did you know her?"

Holly shook her head. "The Wadfords moved out of town long before I got here. They just like the church, so they drive over from Tupper Lake every Sunday. Sometimes after service, they stop in for breakfast. Sadie would come with them, so I know who she is—" She paused, then corrected herself. "I mean, I know who she *was*. But no, I didn't actually know her."

"Neither did I," Stone replied. "But now I have to do her funeral."

Holly winced. "That's rough." She reached over and patted his arm. "But I'm sure you'll think of the right thing to say."

"That's the problem," Stone said. "A young girl is dead. There is no right thing to say."

"I thought at times like this, you preachers always just said something about the Lord working in mysterious ways."

"I became a preacher to help people," Stone replied. "If I wanted to shovel bullshit, I would've become a farm boy."

Holly smiled. "Well, you already have the hat for it."

Stone grinned. "It's okay, you can say it—you think my cowboy hat is sexy."

She laughed and said, "No comment," before going to check on the other customers.

Thirty minutes later, after he had made short work of the daily special and was working on his third cup of coffee, Holly reappeared in the chair across from him.

"Listen, Luke," she said. "I've been thinking. How about instead of doing this early morning chit-chat routine over breakfast, we actually sit down and talk over dinner?"

Stone carefully set down his mug. He hadn't expected this. "You mean…?"

Holly hurriedly shook her head. "No, no, not a date. Just two friends having dinner."

Stone leaned back in his chair. "Thank God. For a second there, I thought you wanted me dead."

"What do you mean?"

He grinned. "If we went on a date, David White would kill me in my sleep."

She balled up a napkin and threw it at him. "You're such a jerk."

"Now it just sounds like you're hitting on me."

"Do you want to have dinner or not?"

Stone dropped his teasing tone and said, "Sure, I'd like that."

"Happy to hear it." Her smile showed she meant it. "But there's just one catch—we have to eat out. I can't cook."

"I'm sure you're not *that* bad," Stone said.

"Luke, I can burn water."

"Okay, so you *are* that bad."

Another balled-up napkin shot across the table and bounced off his forehead.

With a chuckle, Stone said, "No problem. We can eat out. What time do you want me to meet you back here?"

"Honestly," she said, "I'd rather go to the Jack Lumber, but…"

"Okay," he said. "What's the problem?"

"Well, it's a bar. Wasn't sure you'd be comfortable going there. You know, you being a preacher and all."

"In case you missed the memo," Stone said, "I'm not exactly a normal preacher. Besides, Jesus hung out with sinners, not saints, so I don't think my soul is any danger walking into a bar."

"You sure?"

"Just as long as they serve Jack and Coke, lots of ice, easy on the Jack."

Holly's eyebrows shot up so high they almost disappeared into her hairline. "You drink?"

"Sure. Contrary to popular opinion, the Bible doesn't say you can't drink. Hell, even Jesus turned water into wine."

She shook her head with a wry smile. "You're either the best preacher I've ever met, or the worst."

"Jury's still out." He drained the last of his coffee, set down his mug, and asked, "So what time should I meet you at the Jack Lumber?"

"Does seven o'clock work for you?"

Stone nodded. "It's a date."

Holly smiled. "Except it's not."

"Exactly."

As he watched her walk away, Stone admitted he was mildly disappointed that it wasn't a date. But he also knew it was for the best. He hadn't been with anyone since Theresa left him and something deep down inside knew his heart wasn't ready for any romantic entanglements.

Then again, he also knew that sometimes the heart has a mind of its own.

EIGHT

THE JACK LUMBER Bar was located on Whisper Falls' main drag, sandwiched between a furniture store on one side and a liquor shop on the other. There were other bars in town but the locals preferred this one, leaving the competing saloons to make a living off the tourists.

He found a spot in the small parking lot that occupied the middle of downtown, slotting the Blazer between a soccer mom minivan and an olive-drab Chevy pickup truck with oversized tires, fake smokestacks, and an auxiliary fuel tank.

As he walked down the street toward the Jack Lumber, he took in the holiday decorations adorning the storefronts and lampposts. They were like the town itself —simple and homey. Some of the Christmas lights were blinking as he passed by, brightening the night with low-wattage bursts of white, red, and blue.

A brisk wind swept down off the mountains and funneled into the artificial canyon created by the buildings on Main Street. Snowflakes swirled on the breeze and peppered his face as he lowered his head, using his hat brim to block the elements. The cold stung his ears and he wondered if he should trade his cowboy hat for something more winter appropriate. Then again, you could take the man out of Texas, but you couldn't take Texas out of the man.

Stepping into the warmth of the Jack Lumber was a welcome relief from the December weather outside. The snowflakes dusting his hat and coat melted almost instantly as he gazed around the room, surveying the establishment. This was his first time here. As the new preacher in town, he hadn't bothered checking out the local watering hole yet.

The Jack Lumber Bar was long and narrow, with booths running down the right-side wall, stopping when they reached a small dance floor. A well-stocked bar ran down the left side. In the back, beyond the dance floor, appeared to be a kitchen/grill area, with a couple of high-top tables perched on either side of a jukebox. Classic rock cranked from the speakers and while Stone was more of an '80s metal fan himself, a little Creedence Clearwater Revival never hurt anyone.

The décor was exactly what he had expected. Lumberjack paraphernalia covered the walls, everything from old photos to newspaper clippings to actual antique saws. The furniture—booths, tables, stools—was all carved from rough-hewn timber. The wide maple planks on the floor were worn smooth by the passage of time and countless feet.

Stone was ten minutes early, but Holly had still beat him here. She waved at him from one of the booths directly across from the bar. He made a mental note to arrive earlier next time. Assuming there *was* a next time.

As he walked over, he noticed four rough-looking men bellied up to the bar, their attire a ramshackle mix of camouflage jackets, tactical pants, and combat boots. The oldest-looking one pounded on the bar and demanded another drink in a voice way too loud for the close confines of the bar. He peppered his demands with language that Stone's deceased grandmother would have called "colorful."

The bartender, a black man with thick scars striping diagonally across his face, looked to be at least in his seventies. But he also looked like someone who took no crap and knew how to handle difficult people. He set another bottle in front of the loudmouth and said, "This one's on the house, Carl, but only if you turn down the volume and keep it PG-13."

"Thanks, Griz," Stone heard the man—Carl—say. "Sorry 'bout that."

"Don't be sorry. Just don't do it no more."

Stone slid into the booth across from Holly and nodded toward the bar. "Front row seat to all the action."

"Don't worry," Holly said. "Grizzle can handle it. He's been behind that bar for nearly fifty years."

She looked good. Not dolled up, still casual, but it was the first time Stone had seen her outside the diner. She had loosened her hair from the ponytail and applied subtle eyeliner that made her blue eyes absolutely sparkle. She wore a simple black blouse with the silver cross dangling from her neck. Stone had never seen her without that necklace. Clearly it meant something to her.

He thought about telling her she looked nice, then decided the compliment could be misconstrued. He didn't want to mess up and make things awkward. So instead he said, "Grizzle? That's his name?"

"His real name is Skip Travers," Holly replied. "But everyone calls him Grizzle. You look good, by the way."

Stone mentally kicked himself for being an idiot. "Thanks," he said, followed by a pause that was at least three seconds too long. "Uh, so do you."

She smiled. "Doesn't count if I have to drag it out of you."

"You didn't..." He let his voice trail off and then sighed heavily. "Sorry."

Her smile turned into a laugh. "Don't be. I'm just messing with you. This isn't a date, so you don't have to tell me I'm pretty."

"Well, you are," Stone said. "Date or not."

"Thanks."

Stone felt like a blind man trying to navigate a minefield. He scrambled to change the subject, seeking safer ground. "So, why do they call him Grizzle?"

"Because of the scars on his face," Holly replied. "Got clawed by a grizzly bear when he was a kid."

"Around here?"

Holly shook her head. "No, Wyoming. That's where Griz grew up before he moved here. We don't have any grizzles around here. Just black bears and plenty of them, so consider yourself warned."

"Black bears don't usually attack humans."

"Neither do coy-wolves," Holly replied. "But that's not doing Sadie Wadford much good right about now, is it?"

Stone tried not to think about the dead girl's savaged corpse. "Point taken," he said. "You ready for a drink?"

"Thought you'd never ask."

Stone headed to the bar, giving the rowdy men a wide berth. He could feel them staring at him but kept his gaze averted. Much like dealing with wild animals, establishing eye contact with drunk boys spoiling for a fight could be interpreted as a sign of aggression. He was no pacifist preacher—Jesus said turn the other cheek, not take a beating—but he also saw no reason to provoke them.

Grizzle wandered over. "What can I get ya, stranger?"

"One margarita and one Jack and Coke, easy on the Jack, extra ice."

The bartender blinked at him. "What the hell kind of drink is that?"

"A margarita? I think you start with tequila, then—"

Grizzle's eyes narrowed in his scarred, weathered face as he interrupted. "You smartassin' me, son?"

Stone grinned. "Maybe."

The bartender remained stern and silent for several seconds, then broke out in a big, white-toothed grin. "Ain't nothing wrong with a little smartass, long as you realize a little goes a long way."

"That it does," Stone agreed.

"Still don't explain the drink though. Sounds like a sissy drink to me."

"It's not a sissy drink, it's a preacher's drink."

Grizzle nodded like it all made sense now. "You're Stone, the new *padre*."

"Well, *padre* usually refers to a Catholic priest and I'm not Catholic, but yeah."

"What are you then?"

"Still trying to figure that out."

"Aren't we all?" Grizzle said. "I'm seventy-four years-old and I'm still trying to figure that out." He grabbed some glasses and started mixing the drinks. "One margarita and one sissy drink, coming right up." He winked to let Stone know he was just messing with him.

Stone found himself liking the guy.

The same could not be said of loudmouthed Carl.

"Hey!" Carl's voice was a whole lot louder than it needed to be, as if he believed volume to be an expression of dominance. "Preacher boy!"

Stone thought about just ignoring him but knew that wouldn't work. With a sigh, he turned and faced the man. "You talking to me?"

"There another preacher in here?"

"Not sure," Stone replied. "I don't know everyone in here."

Carl's eyes narrowed to glittering slits in his bearded face. Stone had seen that look plenty of times before, in bars all over the world. Carl was a mean drunk, no doubt about it.

"What kind of preacher goes around making fun of people?" Carl snarled. "They teach you that in religious school?" He struggled with saying 'religious,' either because the booze slurred his speech or because it had more than two syllables.

"I didn't make fun of you." Stone wished he and Holly had gone to dinner somewhere else. "I just made a statement."

"How about I make a statement by punching you in the fucking face?"

"First shot's free," Stone said. "So make it count. After that, it's game on."

Grizzle slapped the bar so loud it sounded like a fired gun. "Ain't nobody taking any shots in this establishment except the kind that come in a glass." He pointed a gnarled finger at Carl. "Second warning, bubba. Cut the crap, watch the f-bombs, or you and your boys can get outta my bar."

"Yeah?" Carl challenged. "And what if I don't?"

Grizzle's eyebrows shot up as if he couldn't believe what he had just heard. "That seriously the road you want to go down, Carl?"

The other three men dragged Carl away before things escalated further. "Sorry 'bout that, Griz," the youngest-looking one said. "He ain't going down that road. Not now, not ever. Dad's just drunk. We'll finish our beers and be on our way."

"That'd be best, Dez."

Stone glanced over his shoulder to see Holly watching the confrontation with a mixture of worry and amusement on her face. He shrugged as if to say, *Hey, what can you do?*

Grizzle set the Jack and Coke in front of him. "Here ya go. One Coke with enough ice to sink the Titanic and not enough Jack to get a field mouse drunk."

"Just the way I like it," Stone said.

"Margarita, coming right up." Grizzle started pouring tequila into a salt-rimmed glass. "I assume this is for Holly, waiting ever so patiently over there?"

"That would be a correct assumption."

"Quick word of advice," the barkeeper said as he finished making the drink. "Don't let David White find out you're making time with Holly. He thinks she's his girl."

"What if I told you it may be too late for that?"

Grizzle sighed sadly. "Then it's been nice knowing you, padre. Because by now the self-righteous prick known as Deacon David White is praying for your quick death and eternal damnation." He slid the margarita across the bar.

"Two can play the prayer-warrior game." Stone picked up the drinks. "Guess we'll find out whether God prefers self-righteous pricks or loose-cannon preachers."

"May the best man win," Grizzle said.

"Amen to that."

Stone carried the drinks back to the booth. Holly took a long, appreciative gulp from her margarita, then ran her tongue over her lips to catch the flecks of salt. "God," she said, "I needed that." She glanced at his drink. "A little Jack and Coke to go with your ice?"

"Hey, I didn't make fun of your drink."

"That's because there's nothing to make fun of." She took another swig, then nodded her head toward the four men at the bar. "I noticed you getting along famously with the local survivalists."

"Survivalists, huh?" That explained all the camo and tactical garb.

"Really just a bunch of cutthroats," Holly said. "They live on a compound back in Sinkhole Hollow Swamp."

"The swamp where they found Sadie Wadford's body?"

"Well, it's a big swamp. Goes for miles. But yeah, that's the one."

"Could Sadie have been visiting the compound?"

"I doubt it. The compound is a boys-only club. Women and children not allowed. The survivalists pretty much keep to themselves and aren't fond of visitors, from what I hear."

"So what are they doing in town?"

"They show up every couple of weeks to check in with their boss, get drunk, and get laid. Or at least, try to." She shrugged. "Not exactly sure who would sleep with them, but working for Big Boss opens a lot of doors."

Stone asked, "Who's Big Boss?"

She waved a hand. "His real name's Mason Xavier. I'll tell you about him later. Or somebody will. He's kind of a big deal around here."

Stone heard the front door open. Since he was facing the back of the bar, he couldn't see who walked in. But he saw the look of surprise, quickly followed by anger, and then resignation that crossed Holly's face. She swore under her breath.

Stone turned to see a teenaged girl—fifteen or sixteen, if he had to guess—coming their way.

"My daughter," Holly explained. "Fifteen going on twenty-five, if you know what I mean."

"They just let young girls into the bar?"

"It's that kind of town." Holly shrugged. "Or maybe Lizzy's just that kind of girl."

Lizzy stopped at their booth and without preamble asked, "Can I take a ride up to Plattsburgh with some friends?"

She didn't even glance at Stone, acting like he was invisible, which gave him a chance to study her. She was tall and slender—willowy, he guessed they called it—with olive skin and raven-black hair accentuated with purple streaks. Pretty, with the kind of fresh-faced cuteness that no doubt garnered her plenty of attention from the boys at school.

"Before we get to that," Holly said, "I'd like to introduce you to Mr. Stone."

Lizzy finally acknowledged his presence with a little wave. "Hi, I'm Lizzy. Short for Eliza. A name I hate, by the way."

"Which one? Stone asked. "Lizzy or Eliza?"

"Eliza. Please, for the love of God, don't ever call me that."

"Duly noted."

"So you're the new preacher in town that mom's been telling me about?"

"That's me."

"Mom was right."

"About what?"

Lizzy grinned. "You *are* cute."

Stone laughed as Holly's cheeks flushed red. "Thanks," he said. "Better than being called ugly as sin, I guess."

Lizzy turned back to her mother. "So can I go?"

"What are you going to do in Plattsburgh?"

"I don't know. Grab a bite, hit the mall, catch a movie. You know, the kind of stuff teenagers do on a Friday night."

"What time do you plan on being home?"

Holly rolled her eyes. "I'll be home by eleven, mom. What's with all the super-annoying questions?"

"I'm your mother. It's my job to ask questions and annoy you. Who's going?"

Lizzy rattled off a few names.

Holly's eyes narrowed. "Uh, none of those people are old enough to drive, so exactly how are you getting to Plattsburgh?"

Lizzy fidgeted. "C'mon, mom, don't make a big deal about this."

"Is he going? Don't lie to me."

Lizzy let out an exasperated sigh. "Yes, he's going. All right? He's the driver."

"Then you're not going."

"Come on!"

"This conversation is over." Holly's tough-mom tone made it clear she wasn't bluffing and that further back-talk would be met with reprisals.

Lizzy's face tightened with anger. "This is crap!" She spun around and stormed toward the exit.

"Eliza Bennet!" Holly snapped. "Come back here!"

Lizzy ignored her as she yanked open the door and fled into the cold, snow-flecked darkness. A blast of frigid air rushed into the bar before the door closed behind her.

Over at the bar, Carl laughed uproariously. "Yo, momma-bear!" he yelled at Holly. "You need to put a leash on that little bitch of yours!"

Holly ignored him and started to slide from the booth. "Sorry about that," she said to Stone. "I'll be right back."

He reached across the table and touched her arm. "Wait," he said. "Let me talk to her."

"You? Really? You're going to tackle a ticked-off fifteen-year-old girl?"

"Sometimes kids listen better to people who aren't

their parents." Stone realized he was still touching her arm and pulled his hand away. "Can't hurt to try."

Holly settled back into the booth. "You want to deal with her, have at it," she said. "I'll order us some food while you're gone."

"Sounds good."

Stone donned his jacket, feeling the familiar weight of the Colt Cobra in the pocket. He scrunched his hat down tight on his head and headed out into the night.

NINE

STONE SEARCHED for a few minutes before he found Lizzy behind the bar, tucked into a small alcove that shielded her from the wind. The red glow of her cigarette gave away her position. She didn't even try to hide the cancer stick as Stone approached. She just leaned back against the brick wall, took another drag, and blew smoke in his direction. The sharp, cutting breeze whisked it away before it reached him.

"Come to give me some kind of preacher pep talk?" she challenged. "Or are you auditioning for the vacant daddy position?"

"Neither." Stone shoved his hands into his jacket pockets to keep them warm. "Just thought maybe you'd like someone to talk to."

"I'm not into confession."

"Good, because I'm not Catholic. You got shit to confess, you can tell God all by yourself."

"So what do you want to talk about then?"

"Your mom."

"So you *do* want to be my daddy."

"You got it wrong, Lizzy. Your mom and I are just

friends. Not looking for anything more." Stone paused and, in the silence, she stared at him as she sucked on the cigarette again, exhaling from the corner of her mouth so that the smoke didn't blow right in his face. That was progress, he guessed.

"But," he continued, "since she is my friend, I care about what's going on in her life, and it's pretty clear there's some tension between the two of you."

Lizzy sighed as she tapped away the ash. "Listen, mom's okay. As far as moms go, she's actually pretty cool. But she's way overprotective."

"That's what parents do," Stone said. "Kind of their job to protect their kids." *Which is why sometimes I feel like a big, fat failure,* he silently added.

"Yeah, well, I'm fifteen, not five."

"She knows that." Stone smiled. "Probably why she's worried."

"No reason for her to be," Lizzy shot back, adopting a defensive tone. "Don't let the purple hair and cigarette fool you. I'm a pretty good kid."

"Didn't say you weren't," Stone replied.

"So do me a favor. Go back inside and tell my mom that."

"Maybe I will, if you answer a question first."

"What's the question?"

"Who is he?"

"What are you talking about?"

"The boy who was driving the car for your Platts-burgh run tonight," Stone said. "The one your mother clearly doesn't like. Who is he?"

"Why don't you ask my mom?"

"I'm sure she'll tell me all about it, but I'd like to hear your side of things, too."

"Why do you care? I'm just a kid."

"Kid or not, your opinion still matters."

Lizzy took another drag from her cigarette and studied him. A gust of wind sent a spiral of snowflakes twisting between them. Finally, she seemed to reach some sort of internal decision. "You gonna tell my mom you caught me smoking?"

"No."

"How do I know I can trust you?"

"What kind of preacher would lie?"

"The same kind of preacher that says 'shit,' hangs out in bars, and drinks whiskey," she replied.

Stone laughed. He liked this kid. "Good point. But I'm not lying. You want to suck on a cancer stick, knock your socks off. I won't tell your mom."

Lizzy cocked her head. "Two people who share a secret are bonded, you know."

"So be it," Stone said. "Now, are you going to tell me about this guy before we freeze to death?"

"His name is Michael."

"How come your mom doesn't like him?"

"Because he's a senior. He's eighteen."

"And?"

"He's been sending me texts that mom doesn't like."

"What kind of texts?"

Lizzy dropped the cigarette, crushed it under her boot, and crossed her arms. Stone recognized defensive body language when he saw it. "You know what kind of texts," she muttered.

"Sex stuff?"

"Yeah." Her tone switched to low-key defiance. "You know, sexting, dirty talk, that sort of thing."

"Usually takes two to tango," Stone said.

"Yeah, well, like I said, I'm fifteen, not five."

Stone nodded. "I get it."

"Oh, really?" The defiance cranked up another notch. "What do you know about it?"

"I had a daughter," Stone said.

"What do you mean, 'had'?"

"She died." Even ten years later, just saying those words hurt like hell, a pain that he knew would never go away.

"Damn." Lizzy dropped the defiant tone and uncrossed her arms. "I'm sorry."

"Thanks," Stone said. "She would've been just a couple years older than you right about now. Sometimes I wonder what she would have been like growing up, the problems she would have faced—like you are now—and what I would have said to her."

"They're texts," Lizzy said. "Just words, nothing else."

"Trust me," Stone replied, "Michael wants it to be something else."

Another flurry of snow swept through and left her black-purple hair dusted with white flakes, framing a face that looked guarded and vulnerable at the same time. "I'm not a bad girl." Her voice was soft, little more than a whisper.

"I know you're not," Stone replied. "In fact, I think you're just the opposite."

"What makes you say that?"

He smiled. "I'm a preacher, remember? I'm trained to recognize bad people and you're not setting off any alarms."

"Good to know."

"But good people can make bad decisions," Stone continued. "And messing around with an eighteen year-old could be one of those bad decisions."

"Like, 'going to hell when I die' bad?"

"More like 'mess up your life' bad."

"Well, it's my life to mess up."

"There are better ways to assert your independence than doing dumb shit."

"Thanks for the advice," Lizzy replied. "You should put that on a meme or something."

Stone hunched his shoulders. He was really starting to feel the cold. As a Texas boy, he still hadn't acclimated to the winter weather up here in the Adirondacks. "Listen, Lizzy, it's been great talking to you. I mean that. And I hope we can do it again sometime. But your mom's waiting for me, so I need to get back inside." He grinned. "Plus it's really cold out here."

"So go," she said. "Nobody's stopping you."

"What do you want me to tell your mother?"

"Tell her whatever you want."

"The truth. That's what I want to tell her."

Lizzy sighed and took a pack of Marlboros from her jacket pocket. "The truth is, I'm going to smoke another cigarette and then head home. Happy?"

"Need me to call you a cab?"

"No, I'll catch a ride with one of my friends. I do it all the time."

Stone nodded. "Sounds good." He headed toward the alley that would bring him back around to the front of the bar.

"Hey, preacher?"

Stone paused and looked back. "Yeah?"

Lizzy gave him a lopsided smile. "Thanks for listening and not being a judgmental prick. Sorry if I was a bitch."

"No comment." He smiled to let her know he was kidding and touched a finger to the brim of his hat. "See you around, Lizzy."

Back inside the bar, the warmth was a welcome relief after the wind-driven cold. The loud, boorish laughter of

Carl, Dez, and the other two survivalists was less welcome. But it wasn't his problem, so he ignored it.

He rejoined Holly in the booth to find a bacon cheeseburger and onion rings waiting for him. The burger looked big enough to feed three men, cheddar oozing down the sides from beneath the toasted bun. The rings looked nice and crispy, dredged in a light, golden batter. Too bad he hated onions. But he would try to choke down a couple for Holly's sake.

Across from him, Holly perched behind a pulled pork sandwich and a pile of French fries. "Did you talk to Lizzy?" she asked.

Stone nodded and reached for his drink. The ice had melted a little during his absence, watering down the Jack and Coke and making it even weaker, but he didn't mind. "She said she was heading home."

"Good. Then that's where she'll be." Holly picked up her sandwich. "Lizzy is a handful, as I'm sure you just figured out, but she's not a liar." She took a bite and immediately drizzled barbecue sauce down her chin. "I'm such a slob," she muttered, setting down the sandwich and reaching for a napkin.

"Maybe we should get you a bib." Stone grinned.

"Careful, cowboy," she warned, "or I may just accidentally spill this margarita into your lap." She swiped away the mess. "Besides, I got it on my face, not my shirt."

"The night's young."

They enjoyed their meals in easy silence for a few moments, savoring the good food and good company. Stone liked that Holly wasn't one of those people that felt the need to fill silence with forced conversation. It was a quality she shared with his ex-wife. Thing was, by the end of his marriage to Theresa, the silence between them had been anything but comfortable.

Stone shoved the thoughts aside. Having dinner with one woman while thinking about another was wrong, even if the dinner was just a friendly one. He owed it to Holly to be in the present, not wallowing in the failures of the past.

"So," Holly said once half her sandwich was gone, "did Lizzy tell you about the boy?"

"The senior? Yeah, she told me."

"Do you blame me for not letting her go?"

"Not at all."

"It's not easy being a single mom to a fifteen-year-old girl. Luckily, even though Lizzy can be hard to handle sometimes, for the most part she's a pretty good kid. She just hates living in a small town and I think that makes her push the boundaries."

"Pushing boundaries is what teenagers do," said Stone. "Part of growing up."

"I think it's worse for her since she's growing up without a father." Holly nibbled on a fry.

"What happened to her father, if you don't mind me asking?"

"He's out of the picture."

"That's pretty vague," Stone said.

"Because I don't like talking about it."

He caught the sharp edge in her tone and immediately backed off. "Forget I asked."

Holly sighed and dropped the half-eaten fry back onto her plate. "No," she said. "I'm sorry. I shouldn't have snapped like that."

"It's okay. No need to apologize."

She studied him for a moment, her face solemn and serious, then seemed to reach some sort of internal decision. "I haven't seen Lizzy's father in eight years, when I took her and ran away from him. Far as I know, he's still alive and well somewhere in California."

"Why'd you run away?"

"Because he was abusive. Beat me on a regular basis." Holly shrugged. "I could take it, but when Lizzy turned seven, he started slapping her around too, and that was something I *couldn't* take."

In his previous life, Stone had been trained in interrogation techniques, which meant he could usually detect when someone lied to him. And he could tell Holly was lying now. Well, not lying exactly...but definitely not telling him the whole truth.

But it didn't matter. Her past was her business. If she didn't want to tell him everything, so be it. She didn't owe him the truth. Hell, they barely knew each other; she didn't owe him *anything*.

So he just nodded and said, "Sounds like you had good reason to run."

"We do whatever it takes to keep our kids safe, right?"

"Yeah," Stone said, "we do." *And sometimes it's not enough,* he thought, thinking of Jasmine's grave in Texas. He visited her final resting place twice a year, on the anniversary of her passing and on her birthday. He vowed that wouldn't change even though he now lived 1,800 miles away.

"So how about you?" Holly asked as someone cued up the jukebox and the opening chords of *Highway to Hell* started cranking through the bar. "What made you give up cactus and sunshine for pine trees and snow?"

Stone answered with blunt succinctness. "My daughter died, my wife divorced me, and I had a crisis of conscience that made me become a preacher." He spread his hands. "So here I am."

Holly looked at him with an intensity that let him know she could feel the pain behind his words. "How old was your daughter?" she asked softly, her voice nearly drowned out by the loud music.

"Seven."

Holly grimaced. "I'm so sorry, Luke."

He shrugged, trying to push back the hurt. "Life sucks sometimes. We just have to learn how to deal with it."

"Is that what happened with your wife? She couldn't deal with it?"

"More like she couldn't deal with *me*." Stone looked her right in the eye. "I wasn't always a good man, Holly."

She gave him a soft smile. "Are you a good man now?"

"The jury's still out."

Holly shook her head. "Trust me, I know bad men, and you're not one of them. Yeah, you've got some demons, but I think you've got some angels on your side, too."

"Look at you," Stone said. "Waitress by day, shrink by night."

"What can I say? I'm a girl with many talents."

Stone laughed. "I think I'm gonna leave that one alone."

She winked. "Coward."

"Guilty as charged."

"Ever think of getting back in the saddle?" Holly blushed as soon as the question left her lips. "Sorry, I don't mean it like that. What I meant is, have you ever thought about remarrying?"

Stone bit into his burger and washed it down with some Jack and Coke before replying. Not to avoid the question, but to figure out the best way to phrase the answer. "Not really. Things with Theresa were good for quite a while—and Jasmine was the best thing that ever happened to us—but in the end, there was just too much heartache and bitterness for us to move past. So between Jasmine's death and the fallout with my wife…well, let's just say that at this point in my life, it's probably best for me to be on my own."

"So no vow of celibacy?"

"No, nothing that extreme."

"Good to know." She gave him another wink.

He shook his head. "You're wicked."

"Seriously, Luke, just because things went south in the past doesn't mean you have to be alone forever. Everyone has the right to learn from their mistakes and keep on living."

"I think after all these years, I've just gotten used to being alone," Stone said.

"You should at least get a dog to keep you company."

"That's actually not a bad idea." The parsonage provided by the church sat on thirty acres of woodland, plenty of space for a dog to run around. Maybe even a horse someday. He hadn't ridden one since Jasmine's accident.

The raucous rock song ended and since nobody had cued up another tune on the jukebox, the decibel level in the bar dropped enough to hear the drunken laughter of the survivalists. Stone glanced over at them, wondering how much longer Grizzle would put up with their soused shenanigans.

Carl caught the glance, his head swiveling to look the preacher dead in the eye. Stone thought about looking away, but he wasn't in the mood to let some mean, blowhard son of a bitch stare him down. Stone kept his gaze level, his jaw firm.

Carl, blood pumping with booze-fueled courage, clearly took it as a challenge. He hollered across the narrow room, "What are you looking at, preacher boy?"

"Nothing much," Stone replied.

Holly reached across the table and touched his arm. "Luke, they're assholes. They're not worth it. Let it go."

"Sometimes assholes need to be put in their place."

"By a preacher? Yeah, because nothing says 'Jesus loves you' like a good old-fashioned butt-kicking," Holly quipped.

"Jesus flipped over temple tables and beat people with a whip at one point."

"Yeah, well, let's get out of here before it comes to that."

"I haven't finished my burger."

"Take me home and I'll make you another one."

"Too late," Stone said as Carl, Dez, and their two camo-clad companions stomped toward them with their boots banging loudly against the floorboards.

TEN

STONE REMAINED SEATED as Carl loomed over him. His son, Dez, hung back a little, looking both angry and uneasy. The other two—one with a short, trimmed, red beard, the other with a bushy black beard—braced Holly, blocking her ability to exit the booth.

Stone regretted his decision to stare down Carl. He might have put Holly in harm's way, something he should have thought of sooner. But regret couldn't rewind the past, so he would either have to talk his way out of this or get ready to fight his way out.

Carl stood there with his fists clenched. Stone saw callouses and scars on the man's knuckles. Clearly Carl was no stranger to brawling.

"Sorry, preacher boy," Carl growled, "but I didn't catch what you said. So I thought I'd come over here and ask you to repeat it."

Holly spoke first, trying to deescalate the confrontation. "He didn't say anything worth repeating." She started to slide out of the booth. "We were just leaving."

Blackbeard put a hand on her shoulder and roughly pushed her back. "You're not going anywhere, lady."

"Except maybe home with me," Redbeard laughed.

"Oh, I'm going home," Holly said emphatically, making another attempt to exit the booth. "*Alone.*"

Blackbeard shoved her back again, this time even harder. "Negative, bitch. You're staying right there."

"Look at me," Stone said.

The man turned his head toward the preacher. "What?"

"Touch her again," Stone rasped, "and I'll break your wrist."

"Oh, yeah?" With a drunken, leering smile, Blackbeard turned back to Holly. His hand reached out, aiming for her right breast.

He never made contact.

Stone exploded into violent motion faster than anyone had expected, catching them all off guard. His left hand shot across the table with snake-strike speed and grabbed Blackbeard by the arm. Stone yanked backward, dragging the survivalist across the table. Plates and food and silverware skidded in all directions.

With his right hand, Stone grabbed his half-full glass of Jack and Coke. He whipped it around and flung the alcohol into Carl's eyes, temporarily blinding the man before he could make a move. Then Stone slammed the heavy tumbler down on Blackbeard's outstretched arm, striking the wrist. Bone cracked loudly but not as loud as Blackbeard's howl of pain.

"Warned you," Stone growled.

Carl shouted curses as he swiped the booze from his eyes. Coke and whiskey dripped from his jowls. The curses turned to a grunt when Stone drove his left elbow into the man's midsection, right below the ribcage where the belly was soft from too many beers.

Carl stumbled backward and Stone barreled out of the booth like a predator unleashed. He felt adrenalin injecting into his bloodstream, setting his veins on fire like it had during his warrior days. As he prepared for battle, Stone reminded himself that this was a bar brawl, not a kill-zone. Bodies on the floor was acceptable but they needed to still be breathing.

Dez caught his father before he could go down. With those two momentarily tied up, Stone focused his attention on Redbeard, as the man bellowed, "You asshole!" and launched a haymaker that swung amateurishly wide. Stone easily ducked the blow, feeling it whiff over his head.

He stepped to the side and hammered a hard fist into Redbeard's gut, where he encountered more muscle than fat. But Stone knew how to generate maximum power from a punch and the blow still sank deep.

Redbeard doubled over, retching. Stone grabbed the back of the man's neck and bounced his face off the table. Wood smacked forehead and it was lights out for the ginger-haired survivalist. He slid to the floor like a loose-limbed sack of jelly.

"Hey!" Grizzle shouted. "Stop messing up my bar!"

Stone wished he could comply, but Carl charged forward like an angry bull with its testicles twisted in a knot. No punches or kicks; Carl seemed intent on a full-body tackle.

Stone let the survivalist get close, then spun out of the way. As Carl sailed past, Stone raised his boot and kicked the man square in the ass, adding velocity to his forward momentum. Carl crashed into the booth Stone had just vacated, banging his head off the wall. Not hard enough to knock him out, but it would leave him dazed for a minute.

Stone turned to Dez, who stood there defiantly but without making an aggressive move. He looked to be in his early 20s, like someone who had just graduated from college. But the rough look on his face and the cruel glint in his eyes showed that the only school he had graduated from was the school of hard knocks.

His right hand kept twitching, making Stone think the young survivalist might have a gun somewhere on his person. Stone's revolver was in the pocket of his jacket, well out of reach, but he wasn't worried. Dez was close enough that even if he tried to shuck a pistol, Stone could readily disarm him before any bullets came into play.

"Listen, kid," Stone said, "this is a stupid fight. Let's call a truce."

"Easy for you to say," Dez snapped. "You just beat the hell out of us."

"Let that be a lesson," Stone countered. "Always know who you're messing with."

Behind him, he heard Carl groan as he struggled to extricate himself from the booth. Dez's eyes flicked to his father, then settled back on Stone. "Good advice," Dez said. "You should've taken it yourself, since you ain't got a clue who you just tangled with. Big Boss hears about what you done, your ass is gonna be hamburger."

"Thanks for the warning," Stone replied. "We done here?"

Dez shook his head. "No way, preacher. If I don't kick your ass, dad will whip mine."

"Aren't you a little old for an ass-whipping by daddy?"

"Dad says you're never too old for a whipping," Dez replied. "Which you're about to find out."

He came forward with the speed of youth and the fluidity of a fighter with at least basic martial arts train-ing. Maybe they taught *Krav Maga* out there in the swamp.

Stone never wasted time talking when there was fighting to be done. He just shut up and got down to business. He also didn't drag things out. The best way to handle a threat is to put it down as hard and fast as you can. Battles that raged forever might look good in a movie, but in real life, it was best to get things over with quickly.

Dez fired a rapid flurry of punches at his face, which Stone dodged and deflected. The survivalist then went low, hooking a right hand toward his ribcage. As Stone knocked the strike aside, Dez's left foot rocketed off the floor in a snapping kick that would have bruised Stone's kidney.

Having recognized the right hook as a feint, Stone was ready for the kick. He caught Dez's leg by the ankle and shoved it toward the ceiling. Dez hopped on one foot, woefully off-balance, arms pin-wheeling as he struggled not to fall.

Never fight clean if fighting dirty will end the fight quicker.

One of Stone's hand-to-hand combat instructors had given him that nugget of wisdom.

He put it to good use now.

A short, hard, chopping blow to Dez's exposed crotch ended the fight. The survivalist dropped to the floor and puked all over the place as he clutched his brutalized balls.

"Luke, look out!"

Stone spun as Holly shouted the warning. Carl was on his feet again, now with a knife in his hand. It was not the kind of knife you used to spread butter. He held it low, the sharp point ready for a disemboweling slash, as he lunged at Stone.

On his peripheral, Stone saw Holly pull out a pistol. As Carl closed the gap, she swung the gun over the table, seeking target acquisition.

The sound of the shot rocked the bar.

But it wasn't Holly's pistol doing the talking.

The knife dropped from Carl's hand as the blast took him in the shoulder, the force spinning him sideways. Tangled in his own feet, he tripped and went down. He slid to a stop at Stone's feet like a baseball player trying to steal home but coming up just inches short.

In his old life, Stone would have stomped on Carl's throat, crushing the life out of him. But he wasn't that man anymore. Sure, he could still kill when necessary, but that wasn't the case with Carl.

Stone glanced at Holly and saw her tucking the pistol back into its holster. He gave her a slight nod, letting her know he appreciated her watching his six, her willingness to go to guns for him. Then he turned around to see who had fired the shot that put Carl down for the count.

Grizzle stood behind the bar with a short, double-barreled shotgun in his hands. "Party time's over, Carl," he said to the groaning man on the floor. "Unless you want another dose of rock salt. Gotta warn you, though, this scattergun is a great man-kicker, but it ain't much for accuracy, so the next shot might miss your shoulder and peel the skin right off your ugly face."

Stone nodded at Grizzle. "Appreciate the help."

The bartender grunted. "Didn't look like you really needed it. What are you, some kind of Special Forces ninja or something?"

"Yeah, sure," Stone said. "Something like that."

"Preacher by day, brawler by night, that sort of thing?"

Stone shook his head. "Just a preacher, Griz."

The bartender snorted. "Bullshit. But I'll let you have your lies."

Stone crouched down beside Carl. The rock salt had torn the survivalist's jacket and no doubt some of the pellets had pierced the skin and stung like hell. Not that

Stone had any sympathy. After all, the bastard had tried to stab him in the back.

"Listen to me, Carl, and listen good," Stone said, his voice low and a little menacing. "You brought this on yourself. You got drunk, played the fool, and paid the price. Now you're going to gather up your boys and leave quietly. If you don't, I'm going to be unhappy, and when I'm done being unhappy, all four of you will be in the hospital. Got it?"

"This ain't over," Carl hissed. "You got *that*, you Bible-thumping sack of shit? This ain't over by a long shot."

"It is for now," Stone replied. "Go home and live to die another day."

He stood up and offered his hand to help pull Carl to his feet.

The survivalist slapped it away with a muttered, "Go to hell," and stood up, unsteadily, on his own.

Redbeard had to be roused with some ice water in the face. He staggered out, dazed and sputtering. Blackbeard left nursing his broken wrist and Dez left clutching his battered balls. Carl left with a hand pressed to his aching shoulder and his lips spewing the kind of curses that would make the devil blush.

But they left, and that was all Stone really cared about.

He went over to Holly. "You okay?"

"I'm fine. You?"

"I'm ready to get out of here."

"Yeah, I'd say that's enough excitement for one night."

"I need to talk to Grizzle for a second, then I'll walk you to your car."

"Okay."

Stone approached the bar as Grizzle reloaded the shotgun with rock-salt shells and tucked it back into its hiding place beneath the bar. "Sorry about that, Griz."

The barkeeper waved away his words. "No need to apologize. Those boys had it coming."

"You want to call the cops? I'll hang around and talk to them."

"Ain't nobody here calling the cops, preacher. And even if they did, Sheriff Camden wouldn't waste his time rolling up." Grizzle grinned. "I'm the law in the Jack Lumber."

"Good to know," Stone said. "Any damages from the fight, put it on my tab."

"You ain't got a tab."

"So start one."

"That mean you plan on coming back?"

Stone glanced over at Holly, who was shrugging on her coat. "She likes it here, so I'm sure I'll be back."

Grizzle winked at him. "Ol' Deacon White is gonna kick your ass."

"He's got no cause. Holly and I are just friends."

"You know," the barkeeper replied, "for a preacher, you sure do lie a lot."

Stone grinned, said goodbye, and escorted Holly out of the bar.

Out on the street, the wind had picked up. The snowflakes had evolved into ice pellets that peppered their faces like the rock salt from Grizzle's shotgun. They both turned up their collars and hunched their shoulders against the weather as they made their way to the parking lot. Stone clamped his hat down tighter on his head to keep it from flying off. They walked carefully to avoid the slippery patches of ice that dotted the sidewalks.

Stone kept his eyes peeled for threats. Carl had vowed revenge and the parking lot would be as good a place as any to launch an ambush. Stone kept his hand in the pocket of his rancher's coat, his fingers wrapped around the grip of the Colt Cobra .38 Special, ready to haul the pistol out in a hurry.

The caution proved unnecessary. They reached Holly's car—or rather, a Jeep Gladiator, covered with a light dusting of snow—without incident. Looked like the survivalists had limped home to lick their wounds.

"Thanks for the escort," Holly said, unlocking the door.

"No problem," Stone replied. "But I'm not sure you needed it, since you're packing your own heat."

Holly patted her side where her pistol rode in a concealed holster. "Springfield XD-S nine-millimeter loaded with hollow-points," she said. "A girl's best friend."

"Well, I'm glad you didn't have to shoot anybody with it tonight."

"Pretty wild first date, huh?"

"Yeah, except it's not a date, remember?"

She smiled. "Guess that means you don't get a good-night kiss." She gave him a wink and slid into the Jeep. As she closed the door, she added, "Your loss, cowboy."

Stone watched her drive away, thinking, *Ain't that the truth.*

He climbed into his truck and headed for home.

Alone.

ELEVEN

STONE SLEPT in later than usual the next morning. The bright sunlight stabbed down from a brilliant blue sky, penetrated the cracks in his blinds, and poked at his eyelids to wake him up.

He happily left sleep behind. Nasty dreams had plagued his slumber, terrible nightmares about wolves and rattlesnakes and dead girls. Like some kind of horror movie special effect, Jasmine's face had been grafted onto Sadie Wadford's savage body. He'd been trapped in the prison of his subconscious listening to wolves hiss with forked tongues while rattlesnakes howled as they slithered through a frozen swamp studded with cacti thrusting up through the ice. And through it all, his daughter screamed as she died.

Not a lick of it made any sense, but that didn't stop his heart from hammering as the terror struck deep. When the dream-world finally relinquished its hold and let him surrender to the pull of sunlight, he gratefully climbed out of bed, feeling the hot, feverish sweat cool on his skin as his pulse slowly returned to normal.

He walked over to the window, bare feet sinking into

the soft carpet, and pulled up the blinds. The snow-covered field that served as his back yard was blindingly white as the sun turned the frozen crystals into a billion glittering diamonds. He squinted his eyes against the glare and saw a red fox scurrying along the wood-line. Probably tracking one of the snowshoe hares that populated the property.

The parsonage provided for him as the pastor of Faith Bible Church was the kind of place that might cause some souls to commit the sin of coveting. Stone had learned that fifteen years ago, a wealthy, elderly member of the congregation had gifted the 30-acre parcel of woodland to the church shortly before passing away. Through a series of fundraisers, donations, and community support, the church had built an 1,800 square foot, single-story ranch house. The driveway ran 500 feet from the road to the front of the three-car garage.

Stone had asked Deacon White why the church hadn't used the property and funds to build a new church instead.

"We like our church just the way it is," the head deacon had replied, then added with extra snip in his voice, "Some people know that the old way is still the best way."

As he stood in front of his bedroom window and stretched, Stone smiled to himself. Deacon White really didn't like his raw, loose, earthy style. Good thing Stone answered to God and not the head deacon, because he was pretty sure that if White had his druthers, Stone would be crucified. Or more likely, burned at the stake for heresy. White would call that a foretaste of the hell he believed Stone deserved.

Since he was getting a late start on his morning, Stone decided to skip breakfast at the diner and settled for pouring himself a bowl of cereal and whipping up a couple of over-easy eggs on toast. He washed it all down with two cups of coffee, feeling the caffeine bring him back to life.

While he ate, he used his smartphone to check *Adirondack Daily Enterprise*, the local newspaper for the Whisper Falls, Saranac Lake, and Lake Placid region. No surprise, the discovery of Sadie Wadford's body claimed the top headline. The comments beneath the article were full of the well-intentioned but still trite "thoughts and prayers" remarks, along with a few scripture verses and poems designed to offer comfort and solace. Some heartless trolls also popped up to declare that if Sadie's caregivers had done a better job watching her, she wouldn't be dead.

Stone shook his head. What made some people turn into jerks? Why did they get their rocks off slinging misery onto others? As far as he was concerned, online trolls lived a pathetic, bottom-feeder existence. As one of his seminary roommates had been fond of saying, *"Jesus loves you, but everyone else thinks you're an asshole."*

He put his dishes in the sink and then dressed for an outdoor excursion. He planned to hike up to the actual Whisper Falls from which the town derived its name. Some church members had confirmed that the trail, while snow-covered, was still passable without snowshoes. But all it would take was one good snowstorm to change that, and they were forecasting a classic Nor'easter blizzard in a couple of days. If he delayed the hike any longer, he wouldn't be able to make it up there until after the spring thaw.

He parked the Blazer at the trailhead and started his ascent. The elevation of the mountain's summit was over 2,800 feet, but the waterfall was located just two-thirds of the way up. That was as far as he planned to go today, since he had pastoral duties on his afternoon calendar.

Checking out the view at the top would have to wait until winter ran its course and warmer weather returned in another four or five months.

There were footprints in the snow on the trail, but not many of them. The mountain was not one of the more popular hikes in the Adirondacks. Stone didn't expect to run into anyone else along the way.

The forest consisted of pines and birches. The bright sunlight beamed through the branches, making the dollops of snow clinging to the tree limbs look like the whitest cotton candy ever spun. Chickadees flitted away as he trudged past and red squirrels scrambled through the treetops where they expressed their annoyance at his intrusion with assorted chittering and screeches.

He took his time, enjoying the solitude, marveling at the beauty of creation. Truth be told, he often felt closer to God out in the woods than he did in the confinement of a church sanctuary. He had a hunter buddy, Mike, who used to say *"The woods are my church, the tree stand is my pew, birdsong is the choir, and God is everywhere."* It was a sentiment that Stone appreciated. Too many people thought God only showed up on Sunday mornings, wedged between stained glass windows while hymns were sung, and everybody wore dress-up clothes. They seemed to forget that Christ walked around in robes and sandals, covered with road dust, telling everyone to *"Come as you are."*

Mike died during a brazen but misguided mission in North Korea. Stone narrowly escaped, racing back over the border with bullets nipping at his backside, but Mike had been captured. Given the black ops nature of their assignment, there had been no political negotiations for his safe return and he'd been executed days later, strapped down in front of an antiaircraft gun and blown to bits. A hard death for a good man.

Trudging upward, Stone felt his thoughts creeping toward melancholy. He could run from his past, but he could never escape the memories. Wasn't even sure he wanted to.

The fallen deserved to be remembered, even if he had walked away from that kind of life. They had done bad things for righteous reasons, but they had all been standup men. Being good on the trigger didn't make you a monster. But often as not, it did give you plenty of demons.

With the ghosts of the past haunting his mind, he soon reached the large, flat rock at the top of Whisper Falls. The shallow stream bisected the boulder nearly dead center before rushing over the ledge to tumble 150 feet into a deep basin. Through some strange acoustic anomaly created by the canyon walls, what would normally be the roaring of falling water was reduced to little more than a susurrating hush, a liquid "whisper," which gave the waterfall its name.

Stone stood near the edge and looked down into the basin below, the pool of water churning with white foam. He paid close, careful attention to where he put his feet; ice and snow made the rock slippery. Even in the warmer months, he'd been warned, several people had fallen to their deaths over the years.

After a few minutes, he moved away from the edge, sat down on one of the small boulders that ringed the flat rock area, and chewed on a granola bar. In the snow beside him, he spotted a set of paw prints that could have been dog, coyote, or coy-wolf, leading off into the thick woods.

Seeing the tracks made him wonder if Sadie Wadford had passed through this area before she died, before the unusually aggressive coy-wolf pack dragged her down. Sinkhole Hollow Swamp wasn't that far away, so he supposed it was possible. Then again, her body had been found down low, in the frozen wetlands, and there was little reason a young girl would climb this high in the mountains in the middle of December all by herself.

Of course, there wasn't much about Sadie's tragic death that made much sense. It seemed pretty clear she'd been killed by the coy-wolves, but why had she been out here in the first place? Hopefully the autopsy report would provide some clarity. But that would probably take weeks, maybe months. Forensic evidence was never swift, no matter how all the TV crime shows portrayed it.

Questions without answers. That was just the way life worked sometimes. Stone finished the granola bar and then started back down the mountain. The law could worry about solving the mysteries of the dead. As a preacher, he needed to focus on the ones who still lived.

TWELVE

STONE STOPPED by this house for a quick shower, change of clothes, and to grab a Tupperware dish full of leftovers for lunch, then drove to the church. He needed to start prepping a message for Sadie's funeral. The Wadfords hadn't asked him yet, but as they were members of the church, he anticipated they would want him to handle the service.

He spent the better part of an hour struggling to find the right words, flipping through the Bible, studying all the go-to verses preachers used to provide comfort when someone dies. But they all felt so rote and cliché. Sacred words or not, they had become hollow from overuse. There were only so many times you could say, "The Lord gives and the Lord takes away," before it started to sound like a Christian copout.

He tossed his pen in frustration and leaned back in his chair to stare at the ceiling as if the answers he sought might be contained in the grain of the knotty-pine boards.

Come on, Lord, give me some help here.

It was an honest prayer, but God wasn't talking right now. Or maybe He was and Stone just wasn't hearing what He had to say. It happened sometimes. Even the greatest prayer warriors faltered from time to time and Stone knew he was hardly the greatest prayer warrior.

He closed his eyes and just sat, silent and still, waiting to see if a divine answer would come.

Instead, it was Sheriff Camden who showed up.

Stone sensed the presence of someone in the church even before he heard the heavy, booted footsteps coming down the hall. In the old days, he would have pulled out his pistol, just in case. But this was a church, and while his parishioners might be tolerant of his unorthodox ways, greeting them muzzle-first seemed like poor form.

He opened his eyes and leaned forward as the sheriff stopped in the doorway.

"Afternoon, Stone," Camden greeted. "Got a minute?"

"Sure." Stone gestured at the two chairs arraigned in front of his desk. "Have a seat."

The sheriff was an average-sized, middle-aged man, with the paunchy middle that comes from too many carbs and not enough exercise. He sighed as he settled into one of the chairs. He took off his hat and set it on the empty chair next to him, revealing close-cropped black hair streaked with the silver of advancing years.

"Want some water?" Stone offered. "Coffee?"

Camden unzipped his bomber jacket. His badge gleamed under the office lights.

"No, I'm good," the sheriff said, then added, "Though I'd take a Jack and Coke, lots of ice, easy on the Jack if you got it."

Stone eyeballed him. "Sorry, sheriff. I'm on duty."

"So am I."

"But since you know what I drink, that means you've been down to the bar."

"Right." Camden nodded. "Which means this isn't exactly a social visit."

"Figured as much," Stone said. "No offense, sheriff, but you don't strike me as the type to just drop by the church for a chat."

"You're right about that. And no offense taken."

"Glad to hear it."

Camden shifted his weight and adjusted his holster where the arms of the chair caused his pistol to dig into his hip. Glancing at the gun, Stone pegged it as a Glock 21, probably a Gen4 model chambered in .45 ACP, a fairly common law enforcement sidearm.

Once he had found a more comfortable position, Camden said, "I gotta ask you what happened at the Jack Lumber last night, Stone."

"Do you want to read me my rights first?"

"That only happens if I take you into custody. Do I need to take you into custody, Stone?"

"Are the boys I wrangled with pressing charges?"

"Wrangled? Is that what you call it? You messed them up seven ways from Sunday, Stone." Camden chuckled. "Wrangled, my ass. But no, they're not pressing charges."

"Don't take this the wrong way, sheriff, but if they're not pressing charges, why are you here?"

Camden leaned forward and tapped a finger on the desk, hard and firm, like a judge bringing down the gavel. "This is my town, Stone. For that matter, it's my *county*. If I want to know about something that went down, then by God, I will ask questions." He sat back in his chair. "So do us both a favor and start talking."

Stone saw nothing to be gained from giving him the silent treatment, aside from some brief, petty satisfaction, and no harm in spelling out what went down last night. He quickly sketched out the details of the bar brawl. He left out the part about Holly pulling a gun since he wasn't sure if she had a concealed-carry permit. Last thing he wanted to do was get her jammed up with the law.

When Stone finished, Sheriff Camden said, "So your version of events is that Carl was playing the fool, you gave him a look, he overreacted, and things escalated from there?"

"Not a version," Stone replied. "The truth."

"You aware you broke that guy's wrist?"

"He had it coming."

"If he'd actually grabbed Holly's chest, I might agree with you," Camden said. "But he didn't."

"It was pretty clear what he was aiming to do."

"Clear to you, maybe."

"Holly will back me up. It was pretty damn clear to her, too."

The sheriff arched an eyebrow. "Oh, that's right, I heard four-letter words don't seem to bother you much."

"They're just words."

"That's right, you're the cussing preacher. And the drinking preacher. And the fighting preacher." Camden shook his head. "Holy shit, Stone, I'll bet God ain't got a damn idea what to do with you."

"Thanks for your concern," Stone said. "But I'm pretty sure things between me and God are good. Right now, I'm a more concerned about how things are between you and me. Gonna be hard for me to handle Sadie Wadford's funeral if you throw me in the slammer."

The sheriff waved a hand dismissively. "Nobody's going to jail. Your story matches up with what Grizzle told me. Truth is, the real reason I stopped by is to warn you."

"About what?"

"Those survivalists aren't boys you want to mess with. There's at least twenty of them living in that godforsaken swamp and they're all a bunch of stone-cold snake-eaters."

"They didn't look like much last night."

"That's because they were all liquored up. Fact is, they spend a lot of time practicing combat tactics and shooting drills. They're better trained than your average backwoods militia."

Stone held back a derisive snort. He'd seen zero evidence of any training. Last night had been amateur hour, multiplied by four.

"Of course," Camden continued, "they won't come at you head-on if they don't have to. Bunch of bushwhackers, is what they are. Whip out some Uzis and blast a bunch of holes in your back before you know what hit you."

"Uzis?"

The sheriff shrugged. "Uzis, MP5s, SCARs, whatever the cool kids are using these days."

"How are they getting their hands on full-auto firepower?"

"They have a Class 3 FFL. Technically and legally, they're gun dealers who are permitted to have fully automatic weapons in their possession."

Stone knew all about Class 3 Federal Firearms Licenses. He possessed one himself, just to make sure the various full-auto weapons in his arsenal were legal. Of course, he also had the personal phone numbers of several high-ranking government officials he could call if he ever got caught in a bind, contacts from his previous life, people who owed him. But he preferred to save those favor cards for something more serious than a firearms violation, hence the Class 3 FFL.

"Those aren't easy to get," Stone said. "And not to judge a book by its cover, but I'm surprised a bunch of survivalists living on a compound in the middle of a swamp were able to get one."

"Guess it pays to have connections," Camden replied.

Stone looked at him quizzically.

"Oh, that's right, I forgot," the sheriff said. "You're new to town and don't know the lay of the land yet."

"Carl and his crew are connected?"

Camden nodded. "Mason Xavier, a.k.a. Big Boss, uses them as enforcers for his various interests. He's got more politicians and government officials in his pocket than you and I have pennies. Safe to say Mason pulled some strings to get his hillbilly hell-raisers the FFL."

Both Holly and Dez had mentioned Xavier last night. Stone stayed quiet, hoping the sheriff would keep talking and give him the lowdown on Mason 'Big Boss' Xavier. It never hurt to know who all the players were, especially in a small town like this.

Sure enough, Camden obliged. "Xavier's the closest thing we've got to a mob boss up in this neck of the woods. Seven or eight years back, some longhaired, hippie-type reporter out of Plattsburgh even wrote an article in the *Press Republican* dubbing Mason 'the crime lord of Garrison County.'" The sheriff's face turned grim. "That reporter had an unfortunate boating accident a few weeks later. Fell overboard out on Lake Champlain and somehow got that long hair of his tangled up in the propeller. Pulled him right into the blades. Chop, chop, chum, chum, if you're looking for a mental picture."

"I wasn't," Stone said. "But thanks."

"Xavier don't take kindly to criticism and he's a big fan of loyalty," Camden continued. "Used to be a biker gang in town that he used as enforcers, but they got sick of the long-ass winters up here and decided to bail out and head down south for warmer territory where they could ride more than four months a year. They all got road-killed by a tractor-trailer before they even made it to the Pennsylvania border."

"Sounds like getting on Mason Xavier's bad side can be hazardous to your health," Stone said.

"Nobody could prove Xavier had anything to do with it, of course. On the surface, he looks like a legitimate businessman. Owns multiple companies in the tri-lakes region, everything from excavation to construction to marinas. Born to poor parents and raised right here in Whisper Falls, he's the hometown boy who made something of himself."

"People do love a good rags to riches story," Stone said.

"They sure do, and it helps that Xavier is generous with his money. Look on any building in Whisper Falls that was built in the last fifteen years and you'll probably find a commemorative plaque hailing his contribution."

"So he gets a pass on his shadier activities?" Stone shook his head. "Same old song and dance. People will always turn a blind eye for money."

"It's not just that," Camden replied. "It's the fact that there's no proof. Yeah, sure, word on the street is that most of Xavier's wealth comes from narcotics, protection rackets, and even prostitution. But knowing he's got his fingers in dirty business isn't the same as being able to prove it. And when the heat starts to crank up, a few well-placed bribes in some well-connected pockets make the investigation die like a daisy in the desert."

"That a confession, sheriff?"

Camden glared at him. "I'm not in anyone's pocket, Stone. I may not be the most ambitious guy who ever wore a badge, but I'm clean."

"Glad to hear it."

"Anyway, my point is that you need to watch your back, because Carl and his boys tend to hold a grudge.

You whipped their asses last night and those kind of guys just don't take an ass-whipping well, so expect them to come looking for payback sooner rather than later."

"Think they'll be looking to go lethal?"

"I wouldn't rule it out," the sheriff replied. "Bare minimum, they'll be looking to put you in the hospital."

"Maybe I should start praying for a pretty nurse."

"I think you can hold your own, Stone. In fact, I think there's a whole lot more to you than you're letting on."

"I'm just a preacher, sheriff."

"You and I both know that's horseshit."

"What makes you say that?"

Camden shifted forward in his chair again. "I tried digging into your background. Figured I would do my job as sheriff in this county, see what sort of stranger was setting up shop in my backyard, that sort of thing."

"You don't seem too happy with what you found," Stone said.

"That's because I didn't find anything," Camden said. "There's a giant black hole where information about your past should be."

"Leave it alone, sheriff."

"Who are you, Stone?"

"I told you, I'm just a preacher."

"Preachers don't have their records deep-sixed."

"Let it go."

"I don't like secrets in my town, Stone."

"We've all got secrets, sheriff."

Camden sighed. "Why do I get the feeling that you're going to be a pain in my rear end, Stone?" He stood up and ambled toward the door. "I'll let you get on with your day."

"Yeah, I need to head over to Tupper Lake to meet with the Wadfords, start planning a funeral for whenever they release Sadie's body."

The sheriff paused in the doorway. "Tomorrow."

"What about tomorrow?"

"That's when they can have the body."

"What about the autopsy?"

"Coroner's all finished. I'll be releasing a statement later today that the cause of death has officially been ruled a coy-wolf attack."

"Report's back already? That was fast. She's only been dead two days."

"This ain't the city," the sheriff replied. "Garrison County isn't exactly swarming with dead bodies, so the coroner doesn't have a whole lot on his plate." He lowered his voice conspiratorially. "Plus, between you and me, there's something else."

"Like what?"

"I don't want this to become public information," Camden said, "but I think another reason the coroner jumped on the autopsy so fast is because he liked Sadie. And when I say liked, I mean he *really* liked her, if you catch my drift."

"She was twelve years old, for god's sake," Stone said disgustedly.

"Don't be naïve, Stone," the sheriff replied. "You know that don't matter to some men."

"He ever acted on his impulses?"

"Not that we're aware of, but he could just be hiding it well."

"Sounds like the bastard deserves a bullet," Stone muttered darkly.

"Pretty harsh thing for a preacher to say," Camden remarked. "Thought you pulpit pounders were all about love and mercy."

"Mathew 18:6," Stone said.

"That a Bible verse? Afraid I'm not familiar. I'm not much of a religious man."

"Basically says if you harm a child, you'd be better off tossed in the ocean with a big stone around your neck so you drown."

"Guess the Lord's not a big fan of kiddie touchers then. I like Him better already." The sheriff settled his hat back on his head. "See you around, Stone. Remember what I said—watch your back."

"Thanks for the warning."

"Just trying to keep the peace. I've already got a bunch of coy-wolves tearing up the countryside, one dead girl who was a long way from home, and a strange-ass preacher getting into bar brawls." He shot Stone a crooked grin. "Last thing I need is a blood feud between you and those swamp dwellers, especially when they've got Big Boss backing them."

"I promise you that I won't start anything."

"Yeah, but unless I'm very much mistaken, you'll damn sure finish it." The sheriff shook his head. "Who the hell are you, preacher?"

He uttered the question in a way that made it clear he didn't expect an answer and Stone obliged by not giving him one. With another stymied shake of his head, Camden departed.

Stone thought the sheriff seemed like a decent enough guy, but he still had no intention of telling the lawman about his past. Some secrets were best left buried.

Of course, Stone knew that in his case, his secrets weren't buried. They were just dormant. The skills he had acquired in countless kill-zones still pulsed just beneath the surface like a vein of molten lava ready to rupture.

He had felt that primal pull when the sheriff told him the coroner's secret. He had spent a lot of years extermi-nating men who needed killing. Hearing that the coroner lusted after underage girls made Stone want to lay down his Bible, pick up his gun, and put the bastard in a body bag.

That's not who you are anymore, he reminded himself.

He shrugged on his coat, pocket weighed down by the Colt Cobra .38 Special, and left the office.

Outside, the sky remained a bold blue, unsoiled by even a single cloud, allowing the sun to shine unimpeded. The rays bounced off the snow with blinding brilliance.

As he climbed into the Chevy Blazer, an inner voice nagged at him.

That's not who you are anymore? Yeah, right, buddy. You keep telling yourself that.

He rumbled out of the church parking lot and headed west. He considered punching the gas and watching the speedometer needle pin all the way to the right, but he knew it was a waste of time.

No matter how fast he went, he would never outrun his demons.

THIRTEEN

STONE SPENT JUST over an hour with the Wadfords at their home on the eastern edge of Tupper Lake, a two-story house with peeling green paint and white trim, located down a side street just past the Sunmount Developmental Center.

Dorothy Wadford hadn't looked young when Sadie was alive, but now she appeared to have one foot in the grave herself. She seemed to have aged decades in just a couple of days. Clearly the loss of Sadie had broken something vital deep inside her.

Earl Wadford seemed to be faring a little better, but maybe that was because he needed to be strong for his wife. He couldn't afford to completely break down because she already had. Or maybe he just masked his grief and brokenness better than Dorothy did.

Stone offered them words of comfort and solace. With no good answers to give them, he resorted to the usual verses preachers had been using for centuries. Falling into trite clichés left him feeling hollow, but the Wadfords seemed to appreciate the scripture, so perhaps there was some comfort in the ritualistic words.

Smiling through her tears, Dorothy showed him photographs of Sadie, taking him through her too-brief twelve years on earth. Baby pictures, kindergarten pictures, middle school pictures, youth soccer pictures, first dance pictures…frozen moments in time of an innocent life taken far too soon.

When Dorothy slipped into the kitchen to brew some coffee, Earl looked at Stone through wire-rim glasses and asked, "Tell me, something, Pastor Luke. Where is God in all this?"

Despite the standard verses he trotted out earlier, Stone knew now was not the time to deliver the same old platitudes. Earl was asking an honest question and he deserved an honest answer.

"I don't know," Stone said. "It's hard to see God in the death of a child. But I have to believe He's still up there."

Earl removed his glasses and swiped at his eyes. "Not sure my faith will survive this, Pastor Luke." He settled the glasses back on the bridge of his nose. "I'll try to hang on. Really, I will. But with Sadie gone, it's going to be hard. Maybe *too* hard. If God was around when Sadie died, that means He just stood there and let it happen. I wouldn't forgive a man who stood there and watched her die, so I'm not sure I'll ever be able to give God a pass."

Stone felt the rawness and hurt pouring from the man's shattered heart. There was no salve for that kind of pain, no words that could make it better. Time would either heal the wound, or it wouldn't. Some people bounced back from a loss of faith. Other cursed Heaven right up to their dying day.

Anything he said right now would ring hollow, so Stone opted for silence. Both men sat quietly, each with their own thoughts, until Dorothy returned with a tray of coffee. Stream drifted up from the three mismatched mugs.

As she doled out the cream and sugar, Stone relayed the information from Sheriff Camden that they would be able to claim Sadie's body tomorrow.

"Oh, thank goodness," Dorothy exclaimed, visibly brightened by the news.

"That was fast," Earl said.

"Coroner didn't want to keep you waiting," Stone explained. He didn't tell them about the sheriff's theory regarding the coroner and his perverted interest in Sadie. Their cross was already too heavy to bear without having that bit of nastiness added to the weight.

They small-talked their way through coffee, during which Stone confirmed the Wadfords wanted him to deliver the message at the funeral. He then spent a few minutes praying with them before he said goodbye.

The fast-sinking sun set the tops of the pine trees on fire as he hit the long stretch of road that would take him back to Whisper Falls. His thoughts were dark and gloomy, the exact opposite of the pristine winter sky above. He found it impossible to deal with Sadie's death without thinking about Jasmine. He understood Earl Wadford's pain and questions, because they were his own.

Twenty minutes later, his mood remained bitter. Up ahead on the left, he spotted the sign for the Tri-Lakes Humane Society. Holly's voice filled his head, a snatched memory from the night before.

"You should at least get a dog to keep you company."

Acting on impulse, he steered the Chevy into the parking lot of the animal shelter. He killed the engine and just sat there, not sure if he really wanted to go in or not. It had to be near closing time for the shelter, so if he just sat in the truck long enough, they would make the decision for him.

He closed his eyes, thankful to have something other

than dead children to think about, at least for a few minutes.

Dog or no dog? That was the question.

Something banged against the window and made him nearly jump out of his skin.

His inner turmoil must have wreaked havoc with his situational awareness. Normally nobody could have got that close without him knowing about it.

You're getting rusty, he chided himself as he turned his head and looked at the woman standing outside the Blazer. *If she wanted to kill you, you'd be dead right now.*

He realized his hand was inside his jacket pocket, fingers gripping the Colt Cobra. It had been an automatic, muscle-memory response to what his system perceived as a possible threat. Apparently he wasn't *that* rusty. At least, not yet.

He took his hand out of his pocket as he rolled down the window. The cold air rushed in to rob the cab of its warmth. "Hello."

The tall, middle-aged woman had her gray-streaked brown hair pulled back in a ponytail, revealing a bony face with leathery skin. She had her hands tucked into the pockets of her winter coat. Her brown eyes sparkled merrily, a perfect match to her toothy grin. "Good afternoon," she greeted, breath pluming in the cold. "Sorry if I startled you."

"No worries," Stone said. "A shot of adrenalin every now and then is good for the heart."

"I'm Franny. Well, Francine, actually, but nobody calls me that except for my mother, and you definitely don't look my mother."

"I think that's a safe bet." Stone took an instant liking to the woman. She had one of those bright, sunny personalities that the world needed more of.

"Anyway," Franny said, "I run this place. Saw you

pull up, but when you just hung out in your truck out here, I figured I would wander out and give you a personal invitation to come on inside. We're closing up shop in about thirty minutes, but that gives you plenty of time to find your new four-legged companion." She squinted at him. "Dog person, am I right?"

"Cats are jerks."

Franny chuckled. "You're not alone in that sentiment. So why don't you come in and see if you're a good fit for one of our canine friends?"

"Why not?" Stone hopped out of the truck. "Can't hurt to look, right?"

He followed Franny inside the animal shelter where a cacophonous din of barking and mewing immediately assaulted his ears. It was so loud in here, he couldn't believe he hadn't been able to hear all the noise while sitting in the Blazer. Maybe the walls were soundproof.

The strong antiseptic scent couldn't fully mask the odors of multiple animals living under one roof. It smelled like chemicals mixed with pine, undercut by the pungency of urine and feces. Not pleasant but perfectly natural and expected, given the environment.

Franny led him to the kennels. As they entered the room, the noise became deafening. Some of the dogs leaped at the door of their cages as they barked furiously, tails wagging so fast they looked like hummingbird wings, clearly excited to see a visitor. Stone felt sorry for them all. This was no way for a dog to live.

"Is there a particular breed you're looking for?" Franny asked, nearly shouting to be heard above the echoing symphony of barks and yelps.

Stone shook his head. "Not a particular breed, no. But I'm not looking for a puppy. Prefer something that's outgrown the puppy stage. Something a little older, a little more low-key."

"I may have just the dog for you," Franny said. "Follow me."

She took him to the last kennel on the left. As they approached, Stone noticed there was no dog jumping at the cage door, no furious barking coming from inside.

"This is Max," Franny announced with a sweep of her hand as if introducing royalty.

Stone stepped up to the door and looked inside. Max sprawled loose-limbed on a doggy bed that appeared to be a smidgen too small for his size, large head resting on his front paws. He stared back at Stone with eyes that were deep pools of chocolate brown. Stone sensed a story there and it wasn't a happy one. The patchwork of scars on the dog's neck gave grim testimony to a past tragedy.

"He's a Shottie," Stone said.

"That's right," Franny confirmed. "Shepherd-Rottweiler mix."

The Rottweiler dominated Max's genetic makeup; he basically looked like a Rottweiler with German Shepherd ears. His brindle markings were sparse, making him predominantly black.

"Tell me about him."

"Max has been with us almost seven months," Franny said. "He was picked up down in Ticonderoga, part of a dogfighting ring that got raided by the police."

"That explains the scars."

"Despite everything he's suffered," Franny said, "he's still a gentle giant."

"So why hasn't he been adopted?"

"For starters, he's been trained to fight. Makes most people nervous."

"Doesn't bother me at all." Stone had worked with enough K-9 units in combat situations to know that dogs trained to attack could be amazingly easygoing off the battlefield.

"Of course, the scars don't help," Franny added. "To a lot of people, they make him ugly."

"We've all got scars. The world would be a better place if people learned to look past them."

Franny nodded. "Very well said."

"Any other reasons nobody wants him?"

"Yeah...this." Franny gestured at Max. "When people come back here to see the dogs, all the other dogs get excited and run up to the door, practically begging to be adopted. But not Max. He just lays there, like he is now, and acts like he couldn't care less. I've never heard him bark, not even once. People come here looking for a friendly dog. Max just comes off as aloof. Add that to his violent history and his scars, makes it tough to find him a forever home."

"Sad backstory, lots of scars, and doesn't much care what people think?" Stone smiled. "Sounds like my kind of dog."

Max lifted his head off his paws, ears perked forward.

Fanny looked thrilled, her smile big, bright, and beaming. "That's more than he's done for anyone else." She unlocked the door and swung it open. "Go on in, see if you make friends."

Stone took just a single step inside the kennel, just over the threshold, not wanting to crowd the Shottie. He crouched down and spoke to the dog in soothing tones. "How's it going, boy?"

Max studied him for a few moments, which gave Stone another chance to glimpse the pain buried behind those liquid brown eyes. Then the dog slowly stood up and came over. Stone held out his hand, palm up and fingers spread to show he meant no harm, and Max sniffed cautiously.

Then he abruptly laid down with his head resting on Stone's boot.

Behind him, Stone heard Franny murmur, "Well, I'll be damned."

He reached down and scratched Max's ears. The dog sighed as if a huge weight had been lifted off his shoulders.

"I think you've made a friend," Franny said.

"Yeah, I don't think I could say 'no' even if I wanted to." He gave Max another pat on the head and stood up. The dog looked expectant, hopeful, and just a little bit fearful, as if afraid that he was about to have his heart crushed. "I'll take him," Stone said. He knew Max couldn't understand his words, but he hoped his tone let the dog know he had nothing to be afraid of anymore.

"I've seen a lot of dogs pass through this place over the years," Franny said. "People come in here and they choose a dog. This is the first time I've ever seen a dog choose a person." Under the bright fluorescent lights, it looked like she maybe had a tear in her eye. "Normally you fill out the adoption form and we run background checks and there's a waiting period. But in this case, I'm going to make an exception and let you take him home today."

"I appreciate that." Stone looked down at the dog. "I'm sure Max appreciates it, too."

He signed the necessary paperwork, paid the adoption fee—along with a generous donation—and then led Max out to the truck. The Shottie jumped up into the cab without hesitation and settled into the shotgun seat. He turned his big head toward Stone and gave him a look that said, *C'mon, buddy, I'm ready to roll.*

Stone climbed behind the wheel, fired up the engine, reached over to ruffle the dog's ears, and then they headed for home.

FOURTEEN

STONE STOPPED at Riverside Pet Supplies on his way through Saranac Lake to pick up dog food and the various items necessary for canine ownership, then drove into Whisper Falls where he stopped by the diner, where Holly was pulling a double. He hoped she could spare a minute to meet Max, but either way, he needed to grab some takeout because he had no intention of cooking dinner tonight.

Max wasn't too happy about being left in the truck, but some reassurances from Stone settled him down. He braced his front paws against the dash and watched out the windshield as Stone headed into the diner.

The Birch Bark was hopping, close to max capacity. Holly tossed him a welcome but weary smile as she shuttled an armful of dirty plates into the back. He bellied up to the bar to wait until she had a free moment.

As he turned his head to look out the window and check on Max, he spotted Deacon White seated in his usual corner booth, scowling in his direction. Stone ignored him. He didn't have the energy right now to deal with the White's judgmental piety or his petty jealousy over Holly.

When he turned back around, Holly was standing in front of him. A few sweaty strands of hair had pulled loose from her tight ponytail and framed her tired face. It made her look cute and Stone told her so.

She smiled. "Thanks. You know just what to say to cheer a girl up."

"Come out to the truck for a minute and I'll cheer you up even more."

Holly arched an eyebrow. "Usually takes more than a minute, buster."

A few weeks ago, Stone would have blushed. Now he just grinned and fired back, "All depends on the quality of the minute."

She laughed. "You're wicked." She quickly scanned the customers, didn't see anyone in immediate need of attention, and said, "You've got two minutes." She grabbed her coat from behind the counter. "This better be worth it."

He led her outside. As soon as she glimpsed Max through the windshield, she squealed with excitement. "You did it! You got a dog!"

He opened the passenger-side door and Max hopped out. "Holly, meet Max."

She crouched down. Stone wasn't sure what to expect, given the Shottie's history, but surprisingly, Max walked right over and licked her face. She laughed and ruffled the dog's ears. "Oh my God, Luke, he's adorable." Clearly she wasn't bothered by the scars. Just one more thing to like about her.

"Looks like love at first sight."

"I would marry you just for this dog."

"Is that a proposal?"

"Don't tempt me."

She fawned attention on Max for well over two minutes before she headed back inside. Stone put the Shottie back in the Blazer and then went into the diner where he ordered a bacon cheeseburger and some mozzarella sticks to go. When Holly brought him the Styrofoam carryout container, there was an extra burger in there.

"For Max," she explained as she cashed him out.

"I bought him dog food, you know."

"It's his first night in a new home," Holly said. "He can have a cheeseburger to celebrate."

"Fair enough. I'll tell him it's from his new best friend."

"*You're* his new best friend. But I'll be his best *lady* friend."

"I'll let him know."

She reached across the counter and touched his arm. "Seriously, Luke, I'm glad you're not going to be alone out there anymore."

He patted her hand. "I'd better get out of here before White comes over and tries to knock my teeth out."

She took her hand off his arm and punched him in the shoulder instead. "You're such an ass." But she smiled when she said it.

They said their goodbyes under the glowering, unhappy glare of the deacon in the corner booth and then Stone headed home.

————

An hour later, hunger curbed by The Birch Bark's greasy-spoon cuisine, Stone poured himself his signature drink of Jack and Coke, lots of ice, easy on the Jack. He donned his coat, carried the drink out onto his back deck with Max at his heels, and got a nice blaze going in the stone fire-pit. He brushed the snow off one of the Adirondack-style chairs scattered across the deck and settled down to enjoy the fire's warmth. For a moment, all was right with the world.

He sipped his Jack and Coke with his right hand while his left hand drifted lazily across Max's scalp, feeling the raised ridges of the scars. The dog heaved out a long, contented sigh to signify that all was right in his world as well. Or maybe he had just really enjoyed that cheeseburger.

The night sky stretched to infinity, stars scattered like chips of ice across the black tapestry. The air bristled with a cold, bitter bite and he edged his chair closer to the fire. With no wind, the smoke drifted upward in vertical tendrils, gray smudges against the dark. They devolved into tattered wisps the higher they rose, reaching for the half-moon that shimmered like a bisected silver dollar above the earth.

As if summoned by lunar magic, the mournful howls of the coy-wolves could be heard in the high country, a primal night-song that flowed over rocks and trees and frozen marshes to reach his ears. The music of the hunt, howled from hungry throats and sung through slavering jaws, yet infused with haunting beauty.

Max stiffened at the coy-wolves' cries, ears pricking up into alert mode. He didn't make a sound, but his eyes, firelight reflected in the pupils, stared intently at the dark mountains looming beyond the tree-line.

Stone rubbed his head reassuringly. "Easy, boy. It's okay."

Max didn't take his word for it at first, but after a half-minute of intense staring, he seemed to realize the baying pack of predators was not a threat—at least not to him and Stone—and relaxed, laying his head down on his paws.

Stone sat and drank and listened to the sounds of the night. While there wasn't enough whiskey in his glass to get him drunk, the lulling effects of the booze conspired with the warmth of the fire to ease him down into a pool of melancholy.

He stared into the flames as they danced and flickered and without really thinking about it, started talking to Max about all the things that burdened his heart, all the secrets that nobody else knew, all the skeletons rattling around in the dark-shadowed closet of his soul.

He told Max about his warrior days, about the wet-work missions greenlighted in the name of making the world a better place, about the righteous kills sanctioned by Uncle Sam. He told him about losing Jasmine and then losing Theresa. He told him about devoting his life to God, even though he sometimes hated God for putting him through hell. He told Max that he enjoyed being a preacher, but admitted that he sometimes missed the visceral, adrenalized rush of combat. He confessed to sins from long ago and then confessed to sins more recent. He told the dog all about Holly, about how he felt something for her, but that he couldn't trust his heart enough to ever let someone back in all the way.

Max listened with the silence of a mute priest, without judgement, seemingly content to just let him ramble. It was exactly what Stone needed. Someone—or in this case, some *creature*—who listened without condemnation.

He tossed back the rest of the Jack and Coke, then ruffled Max's ears. "You listen real good, Max."

The dog looked up at him with eyes that seemed to say, *Anytime, man.*

And then the Shottie's ears went up, his hackles stiffened like porcupine quills, and his head snapped toward the front of the house.

FIFTEEN

NO BARK OR GROWL—CLEARLY Max wasn't much for vocalization—but his lip curled up to reveal strong white teeth set in powerful jaws.

"What is it, boy? You hear something?"

Stone kept his voice low as his hand slid into the pocket of his coat and gripped the handle of the Colt Cobra .38 Special, thumbing back the hammer. Adrenalin spiked into his bloodstream and heightened his senses.

He came out of the chair in one fluid motion, the only sound the crunch of snow under his boots. He scooped up some of the snow and extinguished the fire, not wanting to be silhouetted against the flames. No point in making himself an easy target.

A moment later he heard the sound of a vehicle coming down his driveway. Max, who could hear four times better than a human, had just heard it first.

Stone relaxed a bit. Anyone who targeted him for the deeds of his past life wouldn't just come rolling down the driveway. They would flank the house, catch him in a crossfire, hit him suddenly, violently, without warning.

Or they would sneak in quietly, ninja-style stealth assassins, and try to cut his throat while he slept.

He heard the engine turn off, followed by the slam of a car door. He took a deep breath and exhaled, breath billowing like dragon-smoke in the cold air, releasing the tension from his body. Inside his coat pocket, he lowered the revolver's hammer. He wouldn't be needing the pistol. At least not right now.

The knock at the front door confirmed that whoever stood on his front porch probably had not come here to kill him. Most hitmen don't drive up and politely knock.

Most...

Relax, Stone chided himself as he made his way through the house, Max right behind him. *You're a civilian now. Not every stranger you meet wants to shoot you in the face.*

That being said, Stone kept his coat on and kept his hand in the pocket with the gun. Reckless gets you killed. Caution keeps you alive. He preferred the latter.

The front door was solid wood, but a slim, floor-to-ceiling window ran alongside it, allowing him to see the nervous-looking man standing on his welcome mat. The man saw him looking out and offered a weak smile and small wave.

Stone didn't recognize the guy, but no internal alarms were going off. He let go of the .38, took his hand out of his pocket, and opened the door. A wave of cold air rushed in.

"Evening," Stone greeted. "What can I do for you?"

The stranger blinked at him with dark, mousy, bloodshot eyes set in a pudgy, middle-aged, clean-shaven face. He looked flushed, nose red, and even from a couple feet away, Stone could smell the booze on him.

"Are you Pastor Stone?" the man asked.

"That's right," Stone replied. "But you can call me Luke. Or just Stone, for that matter."

"Don't feel right somehow, calling a man of God by his name without putting preacher or pastor in front of it."

"Whatever makes you comfortable. Mind telling me what brings you here?"

"Got a confession to make. Something that someone ought to know, but I'd rather not talk to anybody who knows me." The man squinted at Stone. "Sometimes it's just easier to spill your guts to a stranger, know what I mean?"

Stone nodded. "Got a name? Or is that too much to ask?"

"Walter Nugent. No relationship to Ted. Though I do sometimes get cat scratch fever." He smiled weakly at the lame joke, no doubt told a hundred times before. "I'm the Garrison County coroner and I've got information about the Sadie Wadford case."

That intrigued Stone, but he also remembered Sheriff Camden's warning that Nugent was a pedophile, or at least a man who had pedophilic urges. Stone considered telling the coroner to kick rocks, but part of being a preacher was comforting sinners. Besides, he wanted to know what Nugent had to say about Sadie's death. He just hoped the coroner didn't talk about any feelings he had for the young girl. If he did, the warrior side of Stone might rise up to overshadow the preacher side and he would have a hard time not digging out the Colt .38 and drilling a third eye between the two Nugent had been born with.

Probably not biblically justified, but he could ask for forgiveness later.

Stone swung the door all the way open. "Come on in, Walt. I'll make some coffee and we can chat."

Nugent kicked the snow off his boots and stepped inside. Max gave him a quick sniff and then turned away with a look of decided disinterest. Stone wasn't sure if that said more about the dog or the man. Max flopped down on his newly-purchased dog bed at the end of the sofa, clearly planning on taking a snooze while the two men talked.

Stone led the coroner into the main part of the house where the kitchen, dining room, living area, and office space were all arranged in an open-style floor plan. "Have a seat." He gestured toward the dining room table perched under a faux-antler chandelier. "Coffee'll just take a couple minutes."

"It's after five o'clock," Nugent said, plopping his rotund body down in one of the chairs. "Skipping the coffee and going straight to something stronger is now socially acceptable."

"Sorry," Stone said. "I've already had my quota for the night."

"Not sure I have."

Stone grabbed a couple of mugs out of the cupboard as the coffee brewed. "Not trying to judge," he said, "but it seems like maybe you've hit your quota and then some already."

"Yeah, well." Nugent shrugged out of his coat, leaving it draped across the back of the chair. "You'd probably drink too much too, if you knew what I know."

"Like I said, not my style to judge," Stone replied. "But I think we'll stick with coffee."

He joined Nugent at the table and set a steaming cup of java in front of him. He then sat down and said, "So tell me what's on your mind, Walt."

"I need assurances first," Nugent said. "Anything I confess is protected under clergy-penitent privilege, right?"

"That's correct. Unless what you tell me means somebody would be seriously harmed if I didn't call the police."

"She won't be seriously harmed," the coroner muttered miserably. "She's already dead."

"Sadie Wadford, you mean?"

"Yes, her." Nugent leaned forward, pulled the mug closer to him with both hands, and stared down into the contents of the cup as if it held the secrets of the universe. "Such a sweet, sweet angel, murdered too soon."

Knowing what he did about the coroner's twisted proclivities, Stone felt his fury start to rise at the "sweet, sweet angel" comment. But it was deflected by the word that came after. "Did you say 'murdered'?"

Nugent looked up from his coffee and nodded. "That's what I came here to tell you. Sweet little Sadie wasn't killed by coy-wolves. She was murdered."

In the movies, the announcement would have been accompanied by a loud crack of thunder and jagged flash of lightning. But this was the real world, so the words just hung there without cinematic punctuation.

Still, Stone felt the weight of the allegation, the grim portent the words contained. "Murdered?" he repeated. "You sure? I saw the body myself and it looked all torn up, like some kind of animal had gone at her."

"Oh, the coy-wolves definitely mauled the body," the coroner replied. "But those wounds were post-mortem. Those damn dogs didn't kill her."

"Then what did?"

"Somebody cut her throat. You can see the marks where the knife scraped against her spine."

"Any ideas on who did it, or why?"

"Not going down that road," Nugent said. "But I can tell you this much—she was raped before she died."

Stone almost asked if he was sure but decided to spare himself the forensic details.

"It's horrible," the coroner continued, "thinking about that innocent little girl being forced to do that with someone she didn't want to do it with."

"She was twelve," Stone said. "She shouldn't have been doing that with anybody."

Nugent shrugged. "Nobody likes to talk about it—especially parents—but plenty of girls blossom sexually by that age."

Stone's eyes narrowed. "Walt, are you trying to tell me something?"

The abrupt shift in his tone, from casual to confrontational, made Max lift his head.

The corner looked startled and fidgeted in his chair. "What's that supposed to mean?"

"I know about your feelings for Sadie," Stone said. "And you started this whole conversation by asking me to keep your secrets. Makes me wonder if maybe you did the raping and killing and came here to get it off your chest."

"I came here because a girl was murdered and I thought somebody should know about it."

"So you lied on your autopsy report?"

"You have to understand, I didn't have a choice."

"There's always a choice."

The coroner looked forlorn. "Yeah," he sighed. "I guess there is."

"Make it right," Stone said. "Tell me who told you to lie."

"Absolutely not." Nugent shook his head so fast that Stone worried the man's bloodshot eyeballs would fly out of their sockets. "Not a chance."

"That just makes you look even more suspicious," Stone said. "Looks like you raped Sadie, cut her throat, left her body in the swamp for the dogs to tear up, and then falsified the autopsy report to cover your tracks."

"If all of that was true, then why would I come here and tell you about it?"

"Guilt," Stone replied. "That kind of sin bites deep into a man's soul and starts gnawing until the guilt is too much and he just has to get it out. When that happens, a lot of people go looking for a preacher, which is how I think you ended up on my doorstep tonight."

"Or I'm telling the truth, I didn't do it, and I just want justice for Sadie."

"You want justice? Then tell me who supposedly made you lie on the report. I'll make sure they're behind bars—" *Or dead,* Stone silently added. "—before the sun comes up tomorrow."

"Sorry, preacher, but they'll kill me if I talk. I'm a coward. I don't want to die."

"We can get you protection."

"From who? Sheriff Camden? Please tell me you're joking. That lazy slug couldn't protect a day-old donut."

"I know people," Stone said. "I can have you in federal protection by dawn."

"Federal protection? What the hell kind of preacher are you?"

"Let's just say I wasn't always a preacher."

Nugent seemed to consider it for a few moments, but then shook his head. "No. I'm telling you Sadie was murdered, but that's as far as I'm willing to go. What you do with the information is your business."

"If I'm going to do anything about it, I need a name." Exasperation honed a sharp edge on Stone's voice.

"No." The way Nugent snapped the word made it clear further pressure would be pointless.

"Have it your way," Stone said. "But this makes you look guilty as hell."

"I'd rather look guilty as hell than be dead as hell," the coroner replied.

Stone was running out of patience. The coroner kept wanting to dance around a full confession.

"You think I deserve to be dead," Nugent said. "I can tell."

"For telling me Sadie was murdered? No, I don't think you deserve to die for that. But if you raped and killed her, then yeah, I don't think you deserve to keep sucking God's good air."

Nugent looked tortured and miserable, something inside clearly eating at him. He heaved out a sigh of resignation. "Maybe you should give me last rites."

"I'm not a priest," Stone said. "Only Catholics do last rites."

"Is there *anything* you can do for me?" The corner let out a haunted laugh. "You know, like give me a quick death?"

Tempting, Stone thought. Aloud he said, "Best I can do is pray for you."

"Can you pray for forgiveness? Do you think forgiveness even exists for people like me?"

"That's between you and God."

"Then let's hope He's in a good mood." Nugent rose from the table, coffee untouched. "Because something tells me I'll probably meet Him soon." His shoulders slumped, making him look utterly defeated. "Sadie was the sweetest girl I know, but right about now, I think my life would've turned out better if I never met her."

Better for Sadie too, Stone thought.

Nugent shambled over to the door, a man broken and haunted. He muttered a farewell and then stepped out into the cold, dark night. Stone saw the bright red of his taillights receding down his long driveway, finally disappearing behind the rows of pine trees. Seconds later, through the snow-covered boughs, he glimpsed flashes of headlights as the coroner turned onto Route 3 and headed...

...headed where?

Stone realized he didn't even know where Nugent lived. He had no idea where the man called home.

Of course, he might not know where Nugent lived physically, but emotionally, the coroner was clearly living in hell. Stone felt a stab of guilt as he watched Nugent's headlights vanish into the darkness. He was a preacher. It was his job to reach out to those suffering in their personal hells.

He looked down at Max and the dog looked up at him, not a smidgen of condemnation in his eyes. Not that he needed the dog's condemnation; he had plenty of his own. "I'm a lousy preacher sometimes," he said to the Shottie, then silently added, *Hell, most of the time.*

Still, right or wrong, he wouldn't lose much sleep over his pastoral failure. Nugent had created his own hell. Stone strongly suspected the coroner had killed Sadie and then sought out a preacher for a pseudo-confession. Word of Stone's unorthodox style had started to spread around town, so maybe Nugent had come to him because he figured Stone would be more under-standing of what he had done than your typical preacher.

If so, he had figured wrong.

Stone had some training in interrogation tactics and Nugent had definitely given off some guilty tics. Nothing actionable, but when combined with the knowledge of the man's twisted sexual hungers, it painted a pretty damning picture.

Despite what other preachers, priests, and ministers might say, Stone did not believe that all sin was created equal. Sure, it all kept people separated from God, but he could not accept that things like shoplifting or white lies were just as evil as child molestation. Yeah, all sin was bad, but some were worse than others, and the sin that Nugent seemed to have committed was nothing short of an abomination.

Stone might be a preacher, but he still hoped the sick bastard rotted in hell.

So why don't you send him there?

For a moment, Stone felt the primal pull of that harsh internal voice. Just chase Nugent down, run him off the road, and pump a couple of bullets into his black, murdering heart. He had killed men for lesser things than violating a little girl and cutting her throat.

But no, he wasn't that man anymore.

At least, that's what he kept telling himself.

SIXTEEN

THREE MINUTES PAST MIDNIGHT, the bullets started hammering his house.

Years spent on the killing fields had honed his survival instincts to a razor edge. Sure, Stone knew he had lost some of that edge since walking away from the blood and thunder, but he hadn't lost it all. Old habits die hard and all that shit.

So when his eyes popped open in the darkness, he instantly knew something was wrong. His gut screamed out a red alert and his gut was something he had learned to trust long ago. It had kept him alive more times than he cared to count.

He turned his head and saw Max staring out the bedroom window at the back field through half-open blinds. The dog was clearly keyed up, muscles tense, ears forward. As usual, no bark or growl, but the Shottie's rigid body language said it all.

Something—or someone—was out there.

The moon hung in a clear sky, hurling silver light across the snow and trees, turning his property into a surrealistic nightscape of lunar glow stained with black pools of shadow.

Not ideal conditions for a witching hour ambush, but that didn't seem to matter to the gunman that emerged from behind the large boulder out back. Moonlight gleamed darkly on the assault rifle—some kind of AR-15 variant—as the attacker snapped the weapon up to his shoulder.

Heart pounding as adrenalin pulsed hot through his bloodstream, Stone rolled out of bed. He managed to pull Max down to the floor with him a split second before the window shattered from a burst of autofire. The bullets jetted glass fragments into the room before pounding into the opposite wall. Stone felt shards rain down across his bare skin, opening shallow lacerations. Nothing worse than shaving nicks.

Keeping the bulk of his body below the window, he reached up and grabbed the Smith & Wesson Stealth Hunter Performance .44 Magnum off his nightstand. With a 7.5" magna-ported barrel, the Stealth Hunter was far too big for everyday carry, but it was Stone's favorite gun and the one he kept beside him at night for personal protection.

Bullets continued to pound the house as he low-crawled toward the bedroom's exit, Max scooching along beside him. The dog gave him a look that seemed to say, *What the hell kind of forever home is this?*

More glass shattered at the opposite end of the house, along with the front windows. They were hitting him from all sides. He couldn't hear any gunfire, which meant the assault team was using suppressors.

Stone snarled a curse through clenched teeth as the bullets kept on blowing holes in his home. The gutless bastards had no other plan than saturating the place with lead. This was no professional, surgical strike performed with balls and precision. No, this kind of spray-and-pray tactic reeked of amateurism.

Slugs thudded into the sheetrock like tribal drumbeats, a violent rhythm of rage and bloodlust. By keeping low and sticking to the center of the house, using the interior walls as a barrier between them and the bullet brigade outside, Stone and Max stayed alive.

They reached the stairway that descended into the finished basement. Stone slid down the steps on his belly until he hit the landing at the bottom. He heard Max thumping down the stairs behind him in the dark.

Stone laid still for a moment, senses probing the blackness. He doubted the attackers had been smart enough to infiltrate backup into the basement before going all trigger-happy, but he wanted to be sure before he made any moves.

Detecting no sign of human intrusion in the darkness of the basement, he climbed to his feet. A large, biometric gun safe was recessed into the wall to his right. It contained a multitude of firepower, including full-auto options.

He felt for the fingerprint pad in the dark. Turning on the lights meant the illumination would spill from the basement windows installed around the foundation of the house and give away his position to the gunmen outside.

He could feel the vibrations as bullets continued to slam into the house. The assault team had to be on their third magazines at least. How many rounds would it take before they were satisfied they had killed him?

His thumbprint popped open the vault. He reached in and grabbed the first gun his hand touched. The familiar contours of the Heckler & Koch UMP-45 submachine gun filled his fist. Despite the danger he faced, a little grin tugged at the corners of his mouth. He must look like a bad joke, standing there with a cannon-sized revolver in one hand, a submachine gun in the other, wearing nothing but a pair of boxers.

Operating blind, he crossed to the other side of the basement, directly across from the staircase. A six-foot long, slab-wood-topped bar had been constructed there. Thick river rock lined the front.

He set his weapons down on the bar. This was where he would make his stand. Anyone coming down the stairs would waltz right into his gunsights. Anyone who managed to make it to the bottom would have to blast through rock to get at him. It was the best defensive position in the house. The only drawback was that it pinned him into a corner with no escape route.

But then, he wasn't looking to run. He expected the attackers to burn through another magazine or two, then move in to confirm their kill.

And then their intended kill would kill *them*.

Sure enough, the guns outside stopped firing a few moments later. Stone double-checked that the HK was ready for lethal action, round chambered, safety off. He clicked back the hammer on the Smith & Wesson .44, the ratcheting of metal sounding ominously loud in the silence. The basement floor felt cold on his bare feet. He reached and gave Max a reassuring pat on the head.

As he waited in the dark, feeling the narcotic rush of adrenalin, Stone recognized that he felt right at home. He was a warrior, a trigger-puller, a gunslinger. He did not regret walking away from it all. But he could not deny that sometimes he missed the old days.

Engaging in life or death struggles awakened something primal within him, something that preaching could never satisfy. Right here, right now, he came to the realization—hell, revelation—that it would always be there, rooted just beneath the surface, ready to rise at a moment's notice. It was Jekyll and Hyde syndrome, a man of faith and a man of war, torn between the two ends of the spectrum. If he survived tonight, he would have to find a way to strike a balance.

But right now he had some bushwhackers to blow away.

They stormed the house sixty seconds later. The floorboards above him creaked beneath their weight as they moved through the bullet-ravaged rooms, sweeping, searching, looking for some sign—a body, or even just a blood trail—that they had nailed their target. Listening carefully, Stone identified creaks coming from four different areas above him. Looked like he was facing a quartet of hunters.

Four against one. These assholes should have brought more backup.

Yeah, his warrior side had an ego. A long way from the humble preacher he had become.

He considered taking them out from below, using the HK to fire .45 caliber slugs up through the floorboards and into enemy flesh. But he decided to wait it out.

Let the clowns come to him.

They started calling out to each other as they moved through the wreckage above.

"Anybody got anything?"

"Damn, we fucked this place up."

"I don't care about this place, I care about him. Where is he?"

"No sign of him, man."

"He ghosted."

"Any sign of blood? Did we at least hit him?"

"Negative, man. We looked."

"Well, look again!"

"I'm telling you, he ain't here!"

"Shit!" A pause, then: "Anybody check the basement?"

No reply. Stone pictured the other three men shaking their heads.

"Well, check it, you morons!"

"I'll do it," someone said, sounding like it was the last thing they wanted to do. "Just shut your mouth and hold your damn horses."

"Henry, go with him. Watch his six."

"C'mon, man!"

"Just do it!"

Footsteps started down the stairs.

Stone leveled the UMP-45 at the darkness where he knew the bottom of the stairs to be. He thumbed the selector switch to full-auto mode.

Time to rock and roll.

He waited to see flashlight beams bobbing down the stairway. It would give him something to aim at.

But no lights appeared, even as he heard the heavy clump of booted feet descending.

How the hell can they see in the dark?

Then it hit him.

The invaders were wearing NVGs.

"Hey!" one of the guys yelled and Stone knew he had just been pegged, showing up as a gray-green specter in the man's night-vision goggles. He sensed rather than saw a gun muzzle rising to take him out.

He fired blind, the muzzle flash from the HK lighting up the darkness in orange pulses. He blitzed through half a magazine, dumping a dozen rounds at the narrow stairway, tracking the weapon through a tight figure-8 pattern.

He heard the meaty smack of bullets slapping flesh, followed by pained grunts. In the strobe-like flashes from the muzzle blast, he glimpsed the lead guy catching a line of .45 slugs across his abdomen before the rising burst tore ragged chunks out of his ribcage.

His partner, trailing behind and not fully descended into the basement, caught the salvo across the shins. Bone exploded like hammered ice. The man came tumbling down to crash into his partner, driving them both into a bloody pile at the bottom of the stairs.

Stone stopped firing and hit the light switch, filling the basement with the white glare of fluorescent illumination. The shin-shot guy screamed and clawed his NVGs off his face. Stone knew from personal experience that having the lights turned on while wearing NVGs felt like a thousand napalm suns exploding against your eyeballs.

The other guy didn't scream because he was already dead. Looked like a couple of rounds or maybe rib fragments had punctured his heart. Both men wore matching camouflage parkas.

Despite everything below his knees looking like dog food and being half-blinded, the surviving gunman tried to muscle his M4 carbine back into play. Stone quickly ended the man's misery—and his life—with a triple-burst to the chest.

Stone emerged from behind the bar and hustled over to the two dead men. Above him, he heard someone yell, "Shane! Henry! What the hell is going on down there?"

Stone didn't recognize the first guy, the one he'd shot in the heart. But the second guy's death-slack face sported a neatly-trimmed red beard and a broken nose from where Stone had bounced it off the table at the bar last night.

Stone grunted to himself. At least now he knew who he was dealing with. Sheriff Camden had been right. The survivalists wanted payback. Trying to kill him for kicking their asses in a bar fight seemed a bit extreme, but some men don't know how to take a loss and move on.

Instead, they had escalated from bare knuckles to hot bullets.

Stone didn't intend to give them a second chance.

He stepped back from the corpses. By his estimate, two attackers remained. He doubted they would come downstairs now, and who could blame them?

So he would have to carry the fight to them.

A floorboard creaked directly above him.

Stone raised the UMP and fired the remaining rounds right up through the floor. The slugs drilled through the drop-ceiling and tore apart the wood in a flurry of splinters before punching into the room above. An agonized shriek let him know he'd struck flesh.

"Hell with this!" he heard someone yelp, followed by the sound of hurried footsteps racing toward the front door.

Stone had no intention of letting them get away. He tossed aside the empty submachine gun, grabbed his Smith & Wesson revolver, and raced up the utility stairs that led into the garage attached to the north side of the house.

The garage wasn't heated and the cold hit him as he exited the basement. The concrete felt like a sheet of ice under his bare feet. Gooseflesh crawled across his skin but he barely felt it due to all the adrenalin pumping hot through his system.

Through the glass in the pedestrian door, he spotted the survivalist dashing straight down his driveway, fifty yards away, a black shadow in the silver moonlight. Probably had a vehicle parked off the road, maybe even a getaway driver.

Stone opened the door, raised the .44 Magnum, and gave the man one chance to live.

"Freeze!" he roared, his expelled breath looking like a jet-stream of dragon-smoke in the winter air.

The survivalist spun and fired from the hip, the sound suppressor reducing the shots to little more than muffled coughs. The burst flew wide, tearing up geysers of snow several yards to Stone's left.

Fifty yards was well within range of the Magnum's 7.5-inch barrel. Stone proved it by dropping the hammer on a round that crunched into the gunner's mouth and blew off half his head. The body flipped backward as brain matter and blood rained down on the snow like grisly confetti.

Stone left the corpse where it fell and headed back inside to check on the man he had shot through the floorboards.

He found him dead next to the dining room table. The floor around him was all chewed up from being blasted from below, holes ripped through the vinyl tiles and splinters everywhere. The .45 caliber slugs had shredded his inner thighs, smashed open his pelvis, and burrowed up into his guts. All in all, a damn hard way to die.

No sign of Carl. Looked like the survivalist leader believed in sending minions to do his dirty work. It made Stone like him even less. Real leaders led from the front, not the rear. They ate the same mud, drank the same blood, and swallowed the same shit as their soldiers. Sending men to die to avenge your bruised ego while you sat back and watched from afar was the very definition of cowardice.

But then, Carl had not been expecting his men to die. He had been expecting *Stone* to die. Carl had not even expected resistance or he would have outfitted his strike team in body armor. He had underestimated Stone for a second time. Stone doubted he would make the same mistake again, nor was he foolish enough to think this nasty little blood-feud was finished. If Carl had been pissed about losing a bar brawl, then four dead bodies was going to send him right over the edge.

Stone whistled and Max bounded up the stairs, nonplussed by all the recent noise and chaos. The dog glanced at the corpse and the bullet-riddled wreckage of the house, then gave Stone a look that seemed to say, *Ho-hum. Can I have a biscuit?*

Stone reached down and ruffled the Shottie's ears. "Hell of a first night in your new home, hey, buddy?"

He went into the bedroom and got dressed, putting on a pair of hiking boots to protect his feet from all the broken glass. He made Max wait for him on the bed to prevent the dog's paws from getting sliced up. The dog flopped down on the bullet-torn sheets while Stone made a quick tour of the house.

There were hundreds of holes punched in the walls and every window was shattered. The winter air flowed in unimpeded; he could hear the furnace in the basement cranking out the heat in an effort to combat the sudden drop in the house's temperature, but it was a losing battle.

The furniture had been destroyed by the fusillades. The kitchen cabinets were a splintered mess, the doors flung open to reveal shattered dishes. The flat-screen TV still hung on the living room wall, but instead of pixels it now displayed a mess of black bullet holes that turned the screen into a spider-webbed mess.

Everywhere he walked, the detritus crunched under-foot. They hadn't bothered to shoot up the garage, so aside from a handful of stray bullets, that structure remained intact. His Chevy Blazer appeared to be unscathed, thank God for small favors. But the house? Yeah, the house was uninhabitable. He hoped his home-owner's insurance covered assassination attempts.

As he surveyed the damage, Stone felt the adrenalin

receding from his body, the cold fury of the warrior retreating. He was once again just a preacher, back to normal. But then, he had to ask himself, what was normal? He was stunned by how quickly he had reverted to his old ways, how easily the steel-nerved trigger-puller had come back. Maybe the warrior was his true self while the preacher was just a façade.

But as quickly as the thought came, he just as quickly shut it down. He might have been *trained* to be a gunslinger, but he *chose* to be something else. He could not, *would not*, let his past define him. He had walked away from that life for a reason and that reason still mattered. His warrior persona might surface when necessary but it was no longer the primary facet of his identity.

At least, that's what he kept telling himself.

SEVENTEEN

AN HOUR LATER, Stone was already sick of all the questions.

"Okay." Deputy Cade Valentine looked down at the information he had scribbled on his notepad. "Let's go over the course of events one more time."

"Why?" Stone asked.

"Because I need to make sure I got it straight."

"If you don't have it straight after I've already gone over it three times, I'm not sure a fourth is going to make any difference."

The deputy glanced up from his notes, a red flush seeping across his youthful face to match the red hair under his hat. "Hey, buster," he said, "I'm in charge here, not you. Given the circumstances, I would expect a little more cooperation out of you."

"I did cooperate," Stone replied. "Three times." He sighed. "Listen, Cade—"

The young officer cut him off. "Not Cade. Deputy Valentine. This is an official police investigation, not a social call. I'd appreciate if you'd address me properly."

Great, Stone thought. *A quick-tempered rookie with a gun and a badge and an inflated sense of self-importance.*

"Sorry...Deputy. But like I was trying to say, it's getting late and I'd like to get a little shut-eye before morning."

Deputy Valentine stared at him. "Really? After what just went down? You killed four men, for god's sake! How can you sleep after that?"

"On my stomach, preferably with a flat pillow."

"Smartass? That's what I get from you, preacher?"

Stone shrugged. "I'm tired and getting cranky. Brings out the best in me."

They were sitting at the bar in his basement because it was still warm down here, unlike the rest of the house. Upstairs he could hear the tromping of feet as various emergency personnel went about their business of collecting evidence and body-bagging corpses. A medic had offered to clean up his cuts from the flying glass, but Stone waved him off.

Outside, the night would be a kaleidoscopic mixture of red and blue lights. At least they had turned off their sirens when they got here. The banshee wails had been loud enough to wake the dead.

"I gotta say," said Valentine, "you look pretty cool, calm, and collected for a guy who just sent four men to hell. Most people would be sitting there shaking like a leaf with a piss-stain on the front of their pants."

"I can piss myself, if it'll make you feel better."

The deputy ignored him and studied his notes again.

"Listen," Stone said, "is there any chance we can get Sheriff Camden over here?"

Valentine looked up and smiled smugly. "Negative. You have to deal with me. Sheriff's tied up at another crime scene."

"Something bigger than this?"

"Suicide," the deputy replied. "County coroner killed himself tonight."

Dammit! Stone felt guilt stab through him like a dull knife. He should have done more to help Nugent instead of being so judgmental. *The poor bastard actually went through with it.*

"So," Valentine continued, "like I said, you have to deal with me."

Stone relented, letting go of his stubbornness and relaying once again what had gone down here tonight. He took his time to make sure the deputy got all the details he needed. He didn't want to have to repeat himself a fifth time.

Stone knew that by forcing him to repeat the story multiple times, Valentine was checking for inconsistencies. It was a classic technique, Interrogation 101, designed to show whether or not the subject was lying. Because lies are harder to remember than the truth, most people stumble over them.

So knowing the deputy was just doing his job, Stone played along. Sleep was overrated anyway.

When he finished running through the tale for the fourth time, Valentine finally seemed satisfied. He flipped his notebook closed and nodded his head. "Looks like I got everything I need, so I think we're good here."

About time, Stone thought, but kept it to himself.

"I'm guessing you're not staying here tonight," Valentine said.

"You guessed right," Stone replied with a rueful smile. "The new ventilation system in my house leaves something to be desired."

"Want me to call a hotel, get you set up with a room?" the deputy asked, proving he did have a helpful side.

"No, thanks," said Stone. "I'll crash at the church."

"Okay then." Valentine tapped his notepad against

the top of the bar. "I'm sure the sheriff will touch base with you tomorrow and we'll keep you updated on how the investigation is proceeding."

"What's to investigate? Seems pretty cut and dried to me. I whipped those boys last night, so tonight they tried to kill me, and I defended myself. Case closed."

"Not that simple," the deputy said. "But I think you know that already."

"I get it. You've got a job to do."

"Yeah, if he'll let me," Valentine muttered. Then, realizing he had said too much, he shook his head. "Sorry, disregard that last."

"You talking about Mason Xavier?" Stone asked.

The deputy shot him a back-off look. "All I'm saying is this: whether or not we have enough to make an arrest remains to be seen. But regardless of that, Carl and his swamp rats won't be done with this grudge they've got against you. You kicked their butts and they tried to murder you. Just imagine what they're going to do now that you've put four of them in body bags."

"I appreciate the warning, but I can handle myself."

"Clearly," Valentine said. "All I'm saying is, watch your six, preacher."

"I will."

The deputy nodded, tucked his notepad into his coat pocket, and headed upstairs.

Stone poured himself a Jack and Coke, lots of ice, easy on the Jack, and drank it slow. He didn't usually indulge in two drinks in the same night but figured almost getting killed warranted an exception.

Max sprawled on the floor at his feet, snoring quietly, feet twitching as he chased something through his dreams. Nobody came down to bother him and by the time he finished his whiskey, everyone had left. In the aftermath of the violence and chaos, the house seemed still and quiet.

Stone gathered some clothes, toiletries, dog food—and weapons—and headed for the church. It felt like running, but he didn't have a choice. He couldn't stay here. The house was just too damaged.

He prayed the survivalists wouldn't be foolish enough to try hitting him at the church.

Because if they did, he would turn the house of God into a hell-zone.

EIGHTEEN

THE COUCH in his church office was a little short for his six-foot, wide-shouldered frame and only slightly less hard than a cement slab, but Stone had slept in plenty of worse places. At least there were no bugs, snakes, and scorpions crawling all over him. He really despised scorpions due to a nasty incident in the Iranian desert.

He locked the exterior doors of the church, then locked the door to his office and braced a straight-back chair taken from the kitchenette under the doorknob. An old-fashioned trick, sure, but it still worked just fine.

And of course, he had Max. The Shottie might not bark or growl much, but Stone suspected the big dog would tear chunks out of any hostiles who tried coming through that door uninvited.

He set the Smith & Wesson .44 Magnum hand-cannon on the floor next to the couch, pulled a fleece blanket over him, and was out cold in less than a minute. He slept hard, but he slept peacefully. He had terminated far too many men in his past to be haunted by four more. He felt more guilt over the coroner's suicide than he did about gunning down the survivalists.

He slept until 9:00 a.m. and would have slept even longer if he had not been awakened by someone pounding on the front door of the church. Coming out of a deep sleep, he spent a few foggy seconds wondering how the person banging on the door even knew he was here. But then he realized his Chevy Blazer parked out front gave him away.

He shook his head to chase away some of the sleepiness. He usually woke up more alert but it had been a long, stressful night, so he would cut himself some slack. His nerves cried out for coffee, and decaf wouldn't do.

He checked his phone, taking it off silent mode, as the knocking got even louder. Whoever was out there *really* wanted to talk to him. He saw that he had missed two calls from Holly earlier this morning, but she hadn't left a message or texted. Clearly nothing urgent, so he would get back to her later, after he dealt with whoever was using their fist like a battering ram against the church door.

Turned out it was the sheriff. Stone yanked open the door, catching Camden with his fist raised for yet another blow.

The lawman lowered his hand as he surveyed Stone's disheveled appearance. "Dang, preacher, you look like roadkill that's been run over by a logging truck."

"Nothing coffee won't cure."

"Long night?"

"You know it was," Stone replied. "That's why you're banging on my door at this ungodly hour."

"Ungodly hour? It's nine o'clock in the morning."

"I stand by my assessment."

"Yeah, well, we need to talk about last night."

"I already gave my statement to Deputy Valentine."

"And now I'd like you to give it to me."

Stone sighed and opened the door all the way. "Come on in. But I'm not saying jack-all until I get some caffeine in me."

"Fair enough."

Stone got the sheriff settled in the kitchenette, turned on the coffee pot, and excused himself to freshen up in the bathroom.

A few splashes of cold water on his face helped shake off some of the sleepiness and the imminent coffee would take care of the rest. Studying himself in the mirror, he saw that Camden was right—he did look like roadkill. He must be getting old if losing a few hours of sleep left him looking this ragged. Back in his gunslinger days, he could stay up for seventy-two hours straight with no discernable effect on his reflexes.

Of course, he wasn't a gunslinger anymore. Or at least, he wasn't supposed to be. But then, it wasn't like seminary automatically drained all the warrior blood out of his veins. Last night clearly proved that, preacher or not, he still possessed lethal skills.

Back in the kitchenette, he poured the coffee and began telling the sheriff the whole bloody story, making sure all the details matched what he had given Deputy Valentine. Stone really just wanted them to chalk it up to a case of straight-forward self-defense and leave it at that. He didn't even really care if they bothered to investigate the survivalists. If the swamp-runners threw more men at him, he would put them down too. They would either learn to leave him alone or they would run out of men. Stone was fine with either outcome.

But before he got too far into telling the tale, Camden waved him off. "I got all this from Valentine already," he said. "Guy's a bit of an idiot sometimes, but he does take good notes. Pretty sure I got everything I need." He sipped his coffee. "Told you those swamp rats would come looking for some payback."

"A four-man, full-auto assassination attempt seems like overkill for losing a bar fight," Stone said.

"When it comes to vengeance and such, those boys do tend to get excessive."

"You plan on having a chat with them?"

The sheriff shrugged. "We'll see."

Which means 'no,' Stone thought, but kept it to himself. Aloud he asked, "So if you don't want to ask me about last night, what brings you out here?"

Camden glanced out the window. It faced the field behind the church, snow covering the rolling hillocks that caused the earth to undulate its way to the tree-line a couple hundred yards away. The sun stayed tucked behind drab, low-slung clouds that concealed the mountain peaks and offered nothing but dull, gray, leaden light to the world below.

The sheriff's gaze returned to Stone. "Oh, I want to ask you about last night, preacher," Camden said. "But I want to talk about what happened *before* those gunners hit your house."

Stone knew exactly what the sheriff meant, but he feigned ignorance. "Before that, I was in bed, sleeping."

But Camden wouldn't let him off the hook. "Don't play stupid with me, Stone. Doesn't suit you."

Stone decided he was too tired for verbal sparring. He sighed and said, "You want to talk about the coroner."

"I want to know why he paid you a visit last night."

"How do you know he came here?"

"Tracked his phone," Camden replied. "Standard operating procedure during an investigation. Your house was the last place Nugent visited before going home and killing himself. We're trying to put all the puzzle pieces together, so I need to know why he came to see you. Far as I can tell, you two weren't friends."

"Never met the man before last night," Stone said. "How'd he kill himself?"

"No offense, preacher, but I'm the one asking the questions here."

"There's no law that says I can't ask some, too."

"There's also no law that says I have to answer your questions."

"Yeah, well, there *is* a law that says I don't have to answer yours."

The sheriff furrowed his brow. "What the hell are you talking about?"

"Clergy-penitent laws," Stone said. "I'm sure you've heard of them."

"Yeah, I've heard of 'em."

Stone smiled thinly. "Then you know that I don't have to say jack-shit to you."

The sheriff smirked and raised his hands in surrender. "All right, fine, stop busting my chops. I'm sure we can play nice on this one."

"Sometimes I play nice." Stone shrugged. "Sometimes I don't. Almost getting shot up last night and losing sleep has put me in kind of a bad mood, so the odds aren't in your favor."

"Yeah, Stone, I got it," the sheriff said. "Nugent hung himself." He spread his hands out on the table, palms up. "Satisfied?"

"Why?"

"Easy, cowboy. Slow down and hit the brakes," Camden said. "This isn't a one-way conversation. I answered your question, now you answer one of mine."

"You scratch my back, I scratch yours? That the way we're playing the game?"

"Something like that, yeah."

"Fine," Stone said. "As long as you don't ask me to scratch your balls."

"What the...?" The sheriff shook his head. "What the hell kind of preacher are you, Stone?"

"I get asked that a lot."

"It's your own damn fault."

"You're probably right." Stone sometimes wondered how much easier his life would be if he just conformed to the stereotype of how a preacher should act. "Anyway, Nugent came by to tell me that Sadie Wadford wasn't killed by coy-wolves; she was raped and murdered."

Camden nodded grimly. "That makes sense. Turns out Nugent falsified his report to cover up the cause of death."

Stone decided to put some of his cards on the table and see how things played out. "He told me he was pressured to do that."

"By who?"

"Wouldn't say. Said talking would get him killed."

"It got him killed, all right. But it was his own hand that did the killing, because he's the one who raped and murdered Sadie."

That matched Stone's takeaway from last night's visit with Nugent, but he liked evidence to go along with his gut instincts, so he asked, "You sure about that?"

"We searched his home," the sheriff replied. "Found a stack of love letters written to Sadie. Total creep-level infatuation. Some of it was cute in that Hallmark kind of way, as long as you ignore the fact that it was a middle-aged man writing to a twelve-year-old girl. The rest of it? Sick and nasty, going into graphic detail about what he'd like to do to her if they were ever alone." He paused, sighed heavily, and then added, "Guess he finally got her alone. The scumbag even filmed the rape. Found the video on his hard drive, along with a whole mess of kiddie porn. Most of it featured a violent element, if you catch my drift."

"If what you're saying is true, then sounds like the bastard deserved to die."

Stone didn't mean anything by the way he phrased the remark, but the sheriff zeroed in on his choice of words. "What do you mean, 'if'?" the lawman said. "After all that, you're still not convinced?" He rolled his eyes. "Oh, that's right, I forgot—you preachers like to give everyone the benefit of the doubt."

Stone started to protest, but Camden rode roughshod right over his attempt at clarification.

"Well, how about this, preacher? We also found a hunting knife in Nugent's trash. How much do you wanna bet that the blade matches the scrape in Sadie's spine from where her throat was cut?"

Contrary to providing the final nail in the coroner's coffin, that nugget of information struck Stone as odd. "He just tossed the murder weapon in his trash? That seems pretty stupid."

"Oh, it was an amateur move, all right," the sheriff replied. "Of course, he probably realized it didn't matter, since he planned on killing himself after running to you for confession."

"Except he didn't confess anything to me."

Camden gave him another eye-roll. "We're adults here, Stone, so let's talk like big boys. You and I both know why Nugent came to see you. Without coming right out and saying it, he was confessing to the murder of Sadie Wadford, looking to get it off his soul before he went home and did the noose-dance."

Stone couldn't argue with him. It was exactly what he had thought last night. He'd been a little less certain of it than the sheriff, but their trains of thought had definitely been running down the same track.

"I'll give you this much," Stone said. "It certainly looks that way."

"All the pieces fit," Camden replied.

"Guess it just seems too simple."

The sheriff laughed. "You watch too many crime shows, preacher. Most of the time, the obvious answer is the right answer."

"Yeah, that makes sense."

"Maybe you should just stick to preaching." Camden grinned. "Of course, given all the drinking and swearing and killing you do, I'm not sure you're very good at that either."

"Stop by church Sunday, see for yourself."

The sheriff shook his head. "Negative on that, preacher. Me and God got an arrangement. I leave Him alone, He leaves me alone. Works out best for the both of us. There ain't no place for me in Heaven."

Stone didn't push the issue and the two men moved on to small talk while they finished their coffee.

As Stone walked Camden out, the sheriff paused at the front door and said, "One more thing, preacher. Do me a favor and steer clear of the survivalists. Whisper Falls—hell, all of Garrison County, for that matter—is a nice, quiet place to live. We don't need any more bloodshed around here."

"I wasn't the one who went looking for blood, sheriff."

"I know that," Camden assured him, "and trust me, that's what my report will say. But whether you like it or not, you've gotten on the wrong side of Carl and his boys. Be best for all of us if you and them just didn't cross paths for a while."

"I'm not looking for a war," Stone replied. "But I can't help what's brought to my doorstep."

"Not telling you to turn the other cheek if they come

gunning for you again," Camden said. "Just asking you to lay low if you can."

With that, Camden headed out into the cold, gray light of mid-morning, closing the door behind him. Stone heard the sheriff's truck engine start, followed by the crunchy sound of tires rumbling through the icy slush that filled the potholes. Stone made a mental note to have the church parking lot repaved in the spring.

Alone again, Stone went back to his office. He poured Max a bowl of dog food, which the Shottie wolfed down like it was his last meal. After last night's crossfire ambush, Stone couldn't blame the poor mutt for feeling that way.

The office had a private bathroom with a shower and Stone put it to use, lathering up and rinsing away the grime of last night. Now he smelled like soap, not gunpowder.

He turned the water to cold and shivered under the freezing spray for a good thirty seconds, long enough to chase away any last dregs of sleepiness that remained. Then he turned off the faucet, wrapped a towel around his waist, and stepped out into his office to retrieve some clothes from his duffel bag. Steam billowed out after him like a smoke machine at a rock concert.

He found Deacon White huddled in the far corner, pinned there by Max. True to form, the dog didn't growl or snarl, but the bared teeth and raised hackles made it clear that it was in White's best interest to just hold still.

Stone crossed his arms and leaned against the corner of the desk. "Guess I should have locked the door, huh?"

"Stone—" White never referred to him as pastor or preacher. "—get this mutt away from me."

"Name's Max."

"I don't care what his name is!" White said loudly.

At the raised voice, Max edged closer, clearly ready to tear into the deacon if he determined White to be a threat.

Stone decided having his head deacon mauled to death by his new dog in the church office might play poorly with his parishioners, so he let out a low whistle and said, "Max, down."

The Shottie turned his big head and gave him a look that said, *You sure? Dude looks sketchy to me,* but then walked over and flopped down in front of the desk with a heavy sigh that made it clear the dog believed Stone was making a mistake by calling him off.

"Why is that beast in here?" White demanded, brushing at the front of his coat as if Max had actually touched him.

"Max is my new best friend," Stone replied. "Got him yesterday."

"Good for you," the head deacon drawled sarcastically. "I'm glad to hear somebody—or rather, some*thing*—likes you."

It was always like this with White. Pleasant conversation proved to be an impossibility for them.

Stone sighed. "What do you want, White?"

The head deacon moved out of the corner and came closer. Stone watched the man's eyes scuttle over his naked torso. Not in a sexual way, just taking in all the scars that crisscrossed Stone's flesh. Most people who saw those scars expressed some sort of sympathy, but not White. He looked simultaneously displeased and smugly satisfied, as if some theory had just been confirmed in his mind.

"I want you to leave," the head deacon said. "I want you to resign, effective immediately, and leave this town behind you."

"And why would I do that?"

"Because you're dangerous," White replied.

You have no idea, Stone thought. Aloud he said, "What do you mean by that?"

"Really? You have to ask?" White shook his head in exasperation and then bellowed, "You killed four men last night, Stone!"

Max raised his head and gave the head deacon a warning look that said, *You'd best lower your voice, boy, or I'll be happy to chow down on your larynx.*

"Maybe you haven't heard," Stone replied, "but that was self-defense."

"I don't doubt it," White said, though he did it with a begrudging tone. "But that doesn't change the fact that the pastor of Faith Bible Church gunned down four men." The begrudging tone changed to one of chastisement. "It's not a good look for a preacher and you know it."

"Why not?"

"You're *supposed* to be a follower of Christ, and Christ was a peacemaker."

Stone refrained himself from cracking a Sam Colt joke. Instead he replied, "Christ Himself is the one who said, 'I do not come to bring peace, but a sword.' So, you want to try another argument, White, or are we done here?"

The head deacon's face reddened. "You're taking that out of context," he complained weakly.

"Maybe," Stone said. "So let's try this on for size. How many men did King David kill?"

White shrugged. "Thousands, I guess."

"Tens of thousands, is more like it. And yet the Bible calls him a man after God's own heart." Stone pinned the head deacon with a hard stare. "So why don't you tell me again how killing in self-defense makes me unfit to be a preacher."

"You sent those men to Hell, Stone," White said.

"They're burning right now, eternally damned, screaming in agony, and it's all your fault."

"I may have pulled the trigger, but I didn't pick the fight."

"Didn't you?"

"What's that supposed to mean?"

"They attacked you because of what happened at the Jack Lumber. If you hadn't taken Holly to that bar, none of this would have happened."

Stone knew that White had a skewed way of thinking, but he still couldn't believe the crap he was hearing. "Are you serious? So I should have just sat there and let those guys put their hands on Holly? Is that what you're saying?"

"No." White shook his head. "That's not what I'm saying at all. What I'm saying is that you never should have taken her to the bar in the first place."

Stone folded his arms across his bare chest. "So that's what this is really about." A statement, not a question. "All this holier-than-thou, finger-pointing, blame-game bullshit isn't about what's best for the church. You're just jealous that I went out with Holly."

"That's not it at all," White protested weakly.

"You want me to leave town so you can have her to yourself."

"I want you to leave town because in just the short time you've been here, a young girl has been killed, four men were gunned down at your home, and from what I'm hearing, the coroner has committed suicide." The head deacon waved a hand at Stone's scarred-up torso. "You can see it all over your body, plain as day, that you're a violent man, and you've brought that violence with you to Whisper Falls."

"We all have a past," Stone said. "And we've got to learn to live with it. All these scars, they're from my old life. That's not who I am anymore." *Not completely, anyway,* he silently added.

"There's four dead men with your bullets in them that would strongly disagree with that," White replied.

"I'm not turning the other cheek when somebody is shooting at me."

The head deacon sighed. "I try not to hate you, Stone. Honestly, I do. But whatever the reason, however you choose to justify it, the reality is that you killed people last night, and the last thing this church—or this town— needs is a killer preacher. Just do us all a favor, jump in that ugly truck of yours, and ride off into the sunset."

Stone uncrossed his arms and pushed away from the desk. "Are we done here, White? I'd really like to get dressed and find some breakfast."

"Yeah, I imagine blowing away four sinners works up a bit of an appetite," White muttered. But he moved toward the door, pausing just long enough to say, "I'm not kidding, Stone. I want you gone, and someday I'm going to get enough votes to kick you out of this church."

"Goodbye, White." Stone's clipped tone made it clear further conversation would be unwelcome.

"God bless you." The head deacon made the words sound like a profane insult as he left.

With White gone, Stone quickly dressed and then tried calling Holly. But her phone went straight to voicemail. Probably still busy down at the diner, dealing with the late morning breakfast crowd.

He was just getting ready to grab his keys and head down to the diner himself when he heard the front door of the church open. Footsteps—two pairs, one wearing boots, one wearing something lighter, judging from the sound—headed toward his office.

Max pushed himself up into a prone position, perched on his haunches as he stared at the door.

Stone wondered how many more visitors he was going to have this morning. Last night's shootout seemed to have given him a popularity spike.

When the two men walked into his office, Stone's adrenaline kicked into overdrive. He grabbed for his gun, praying he was fast enough to at least get a shot off before he died.

NINETEEN

AS HIS FINGERS wrapped around the grip of the Smith & Wesson .44 Magnum sitting on his desk, Stone heard a smooth, cultured voice call out, "No, Mr. Stone! Please! No guns! We mean you no harm!"

Stone swept the revolver up and around, scattering papers in all directions. He ignored the shouted plea of Mason 'Big Boss' Xavier and settled the gunsights on the second man, standing to Xavier's left and slightly behind, like a well-trained mutt.

Carl, the mad dog leader of the survivalist pack, moved his hand toward his own holstered sidearm. But the look in his eyes said that he knew he was too slow. He showed no fear, just hate, as he prepared to die.

Xavier stepped in front of Stone's .44 Magnum, hands held high in the classic "don't shoot" position. "No!" This time he said it loudly, with more authority, the voice of someone accustomed to having his commands obeyed. "Mr. Stone, it is not what you think."

Stone managed to stop his finger from pulling the trigger about a half-ounce from breakpoint. "Then what is it?" he rasped.

"It's an apology."

"Tell your boy to take his hand off his gun."

Xavier turned his head and nodded at Carl. The survivalist leader reluctantly moved his hand away from his pistol and let his camouflage jacket fall back into place. His eyes were cold and angry as they glared at the preacher.

Xavier turned back toward Stone. "Better? Perhaps you can put down your blaster now and we can all be friends."

"I think we're well past the point of any friendship possibility," Stone growled. But he lowered the .44, letting it hang down by his side, muzzle pointing at the floor. He left the hammer fully cocked. His finger rested just outside the trigger guard, the metal cool to the touch. If Carl so much as twitched wrong, the gun would be back in play in a heartbeat, and it would be one of the last heartbeats Carl would ever have.

"Oh, I wouldn't be so sure about that," Xavier said, lowering his hands. He had the kind of mega-wattage smile that most movie stars would have sold their soul for. Stone found it a little over the top, like a disreputable used car salesman. He wore no hat, revealing razor-cut black hair with nary a strand out of place. In fact, everything about the alleged crime lord of Garrison County seemed tight, neat, well put together.

Stone took in the expensive coat, tailored pants, and the dress shoes spackled with moisture droplets from where the snow had melted. Apparently, Mason Xavier was a man who dressed to impress rather than dressed appropriately for the wintry environment.

Xavier reached up and patted his left breast pocket, looking like he was about to recite the pledge of allegiance. "I'm fairly confident that what I have in here will make us friends."

"Unless you've got something that can erase the fact that this son of a bitch—" Stone pointed a finger at Carl, "—sent four of his scumbags to kill me last night, I think you're sorely mistaken."

"The only mistake was on Carl's part," Xavier said. "What happened last night was an error in judgment and four good men paid the price with their lives."

"Four men, anyway. I think I might disagree with you about the 'good' part."

"How very cynical, especially for a preacher. Maybe you should try forgiveness, see how that works for you."

"Not really my style when someone tries to kill me."

"I do believe Jesus Christ forgave the centurions who hammered home the nails."

"In case you didn't notice—" Stone waggled the .44 Magnum. "—I'm not Jesus."

"Clearly." Xavier heaved out a long, dramatic sigh. "Well, if I can't appeal to your better angels, perhaps I can offer you some recompense instead." He went to slide his hand inside his coat, then paused, looking askance at Stone. "May I?"

"Slow and easy."

"Just the way I like my women," Carl snickered.

Stone and Xavier ignored him.

Xavier, moving at a speed just shy of oozing molasses, reached into an inner pocket of his coat. When he withdrew it, there was a check in his hand.

"I'm unarmed," Xavier said. "I never carry a gun."

"Seems unwise for a man of your reputation."

Xavier's smile never wavered. Stone wondered if the man slept with that cosmetically-whitened smile on his face. "It would appear you've been talking to Sheriff Camden," Xavier said bemusedly. "He does love to besmirch my character."

"He's not the only one around here who says you're

dirty," Stone replied. "Like I said, you seem to have a reputation."

Xavier shrugged. "I'm a businessman with a lot of irons in the proverbial fire, irons which have made me a considerable amount of wealth. People like to spread falsehoods about the wealthy, frequently assuming they cannot have come by their riches through anything other than nefarious methods."

The man's elitism came through loud and clear. It wasn't just the big words or fancy phrasing, but in the tone of his voice, a charming façade that couldn't quite hide the sneer behind it. Stone wondered if Xavier naturally talked with that much pomposity, or if he had cultivated the upper-league educated style to impress his small-town neighbors. Regardless, it was blatantly obvious that the Big Boss of Whisper Falls believed himself better than the people around him. The king who lived among the peasants.

"So, you got wealthy through legitimate means," Stone said, "and the rumors about you are a bunch of crap, so that's why you don't need a gun. That about sum it up?"

"Actually, I have no need of a gun because I have Carl and his skilled patriots to provide security for me."

Stone almost scoffed at the word *skilled*. Was Xavier serious? Carl and his so-called patriots had been bested in a four-on-one bar brawl, then managed to get them-selves snuffed in a four-on-one assassination attempt. "Skilled" was not an adjective that applied. They were thugs playing at being operators, nothing more. But prob-ably up here in mountain country, that was good enough.

Stone laced his next words with a sharp tone. "So, what you're saying is that you hire people to do your dirty work for you."

The smile didn't lose a single watt of luminosity as

Xavier refused to rise to the bait. "I pay them to protect me," he said. "Nothing less, nothing more. Their particular set of skills—though obviously not as impressive as yours—safeguards my interests and that is all there is to our arrangement."

"That what they were doing last night when they tried to kill me? Safeguarding your interests?"

"Ah, at last we come to the rub of the matter." Xavier stepped forward and offered Stone the check, folded in half and pinched between the middle and index finger of his left hand.

Frowning, Stone took the check with his left hand, the Smith & Wesson still filling his right, noting the softness of Xavier's hand as he did so. No callouses, no scars, no rough patches of skin. The man hadn't worked hard labor in a long time, if he ever had at all.

Stone unfolded the check and saw that it was made out to him for the amount of $100,000.

He looked at Xavier. "What the hell is this?"

"An apology," Xavier replied. "You were wrongfully targeted last night. Carl and his crew work for me, but I did not sanction the hit on you."

Carl managed to look angry and embarrassed at the same time.

"If you had nothing to do with all the killing that went down last night," Stone said, "then why are you giving me a check for a hundred grand?"

"Call it employer responsibility," Xavier replied. "Carl and his boys may have been acting without my authority, but they are my employees nonetheless, and sometimes an employer must bear the weight and repercussions of their subordinates' actions."

"Sometimes a man just needs to pay for his own sins," Stone rasped, nailing Carl with a hard-eyed stare.

Carl's lips peeled back from his tobacco-stained teeth. "Just say when and where, preacher."

"Shut up, Carl." The three words spat from Xavier's mouth like bullets. For the first time, his smile wavered ever so slightly. "I brought you here to apologize, not cause further trouble."

"Yeah, okay." The fires of madness danced in Carl's eyes as he looked at Stone. "Sorry."

"I don't believe you," Stone growled. "You ain't sorry for shit."

"Yeah, well, I said it, didn't I?"

"You sure did. Now it's my turn to say something." Stone's eyes went cold and his voice frosted with ice. "You send any more of your boys after me, you'll be burying them in the boneyard, too."

"I underestimated my enemy," Carl said. "But don't worry, that tactical error won't happen next time."

"There won't be a next time," Xavier interjected. "Bygones will be bygones." He glared at Carl. "Am I making myself clear?"

"Yeah, yeah, I hear you."

"Make sure you do, because my tolerance level for disobedience is miniscule."

"I got it, boss."

"Are we done here?" Stone asked. "I've got work to do."

"Of course," Xavier said. "We will take our leave and let you get to it." He gestured at the check in Stone's hand. "Again, please accept my apologies for last night's unfortunate faux pas."

"I'll accept the apology," Stone replied, "even though I think it's bullshit." He held out the check. "But I'm not accepting this."

Xavier kept his arms down by his side, refusing to take it back. "What's that old saying? Don't look a gift horse in the mouth? Trust me, Mr. Stone, I can afford it."

"I'm sure you can," Stone said. "But this isn't a horse and it sure as hell isn't a gift. I know a bribe when I see one."

"I have no need to bribe a small-town preacher," Xavier countered. "That would be a poor return on my investment. But if you're uncomfortable taking the money, donate it to your church coffers. Do some good with it. Put on one hell of a Christmas concert. Pay for some mission trips. Sponsor some starving children in Ethiopia." He waved a hand dismissively. "Or whatever righteous causes you church people are into these days."

"The church doesn't want your blood money." Stone dropped the check. It fluttered to the floor and landed at Xavier's feet.

The movie star smile vanished. Something cold and reptilian took its place. Behind the dashing good looks and cultured speech lurked a monster, and Stone was catching a glimpse.

"Listen to me, preacher." Xavier's voice was not quite a sinister hiss, but close. "You would do well to make me an ally rather than an enemy."

"James 4:4," Stone quoted. "Whoever wants to be a friend of the world makes himself an enemy of God." He gestured at the fallen check. "So take your blood money —" He then pointed at Carl. "—and your trash and get the hell out of here."

The beast held sway for another few seconds as Xavier glared daggers at him, eyes hot and furious. But then the smile returned, dawning across his face like a brilliant sun breaking through the darkness, cloaking the monster. "You're making a grave mistake," he said, his voice once again calm.

"Won't be my first."

"Could very well be your last."

"Somehow I doubt that."

"We'll be leaving now." Xavier exited the office. He left the check lying on the floor.

Carl hung back for a moment, waiting for his boss to get out of earshot before he growled at Stone, "Just to be clear, preacher, I ain't nobody's lapdog and Mason don't hold my leash. You're gonna pay for those four boys you got lucky and killed last night."

"Keep sending 'em," Stone replied. "Hell's got plenty of room."

"Remember what you said about a man paying for his own sins?" Carl shook his head. "It don't always work that way. Sometimes the innocent people in a man's life pay for his sins. Know what I mean?"

Stone clenched his teeth as a vein throbbed in his jaw.

Carl grinned wickedly. "By the way, how are Holly and Lizzy these days?"

Stone raised the Smith & Wesson, pointed it at Carl's face, and curled his finger around the trigger. "Get out of my church before I kill you right where you stand."

"Spilling blood on holy ground?" Carl said. "Ain't that some kind of really bad sin?"

"My sins are forgiven." Stone's finger tightened on the trigger. "How about yours?"

"Guess I'll find out soon enough." Carl fired off a mocking salute. "Till we meet again, preacher."

When he was gone, Stone lowered the revolver. It felt like a heavy weight in his hand, a Magnum-sized cross to bear. He'd come here to start a new life, away from the violence and bloodshed of his old days, and yet here he was, embroiled in a deadly feud within weeks of rolling into town. It seemed like the warrior within him refused to go dormant, the peace he sought nothing but a phantom that would forever slip through his fingers.

He knew beyond a shadow of a doubt that some people just attracted violence. Maybe he was one of those people. Maybe he would be eternally torn between God and gunfire.

And now Holly and Lizzy, people he truly cared for, had been thrust into the crosshairs. He might not know how to reconcile the preacher he had become with the warrior he had been, but one thing he knew for sure.

If they hurt Holly and Lizzy, he would kill them all.

No mercy. No remorse. No repentance.

Just burn-it-down, scorched earth, blood-and-thunder destruction.

He picked up his phone and called Holly, trying to ignore just how much the thought of losing her terrified him.

TWENTY

SHE ANSWERED on the fourth ring and didn't wait for him to say anything. "Oh my God, Luke. Are you okay? I heard about what happened last night. The whole town is talking about it."

"I'm okay. House is all shot up, but Max and I are fine."

She paused, then quietly said, "I heard you killed some men."

"There was no choice, Holly. Believe me."

"I do." Her voice brightened. "Listen, we're swamped down here, but you can tell me all about it tonight. I'm cooking you dinner."

"You are? Why?"

"Because you're going to do me a favor."

Least I can do, since I just put you in the crosshairs. "Sure, name it."

"I woke up this morning to a flat tire. I managed to get a ride to work, but I need a Good Samaritan to fix the flat." She paused, then said sheepishly, "I never learned how."

"I'll head over there now and take care of it. Need a ride home later?"

"Nope, got that all taken care of. Thanks, though. You're an angel."

"Not always."

"Someday I may ask you to prove that," she said, and Stone could just imagine the wink she was giving him through the phone. "See you tonight around six. Hope you like grilled cheese and Raman soup."

"My favorite. Just make sure you cut all the crusts off my sandwich."

She laughed. "Deal. Gotta go, customers waiting. See you later." It came out in a rush and she hung up before he could even say goodbye.

Stone put the phone in his pocket and looked down at Max. "Guess we've got a date tonight, Max. Or more like a not-date. Who the hell knows? Women, right?"

The dog just gave him a look that seemed to say, *Man, I'm neutered. I don't care about bitches.*

Stone donned his rancher's coat and swapped the Smith & Wesson .44 caliber hand-cannon for the smaller Colt Cobra he typically carried. He dropped a couple of speed-loaders in the opposite pocket, balancing out the weight and giving him some extra hollow-point persuasion if the survivalists took another swing at getting some payback.

He thought about going back to his shot-up house to retrieve a semi-automatic option and extra magazines from the vault but decided not to bother. The odds of a broad daylight attack were slim and if it did happen, eighteen man-stoppers from a .38 should be enough to deal with the problem.

Outside, the sky sulked under slate-gray clouds that threatened to dump snow by nightfall. The church sign-board, wreathed in festive holiday lights, proclaimed

"Keep Christ in Christmas" on one side, and "Jesus is the Reason for the Season" on the other.

As Max settled down in the passenger seat of the Blazer, Stone reached over, ruffled the dog's ears, and said, "Any of those dirtbags mess with Holly or Lizzy, they're gonna meet Jesus in person."

Max thumped his tail in approval.

Stone started the engine and cranked up the heat. "Let's find some breakfast, buddy. We've got a flat tire to fix."

———

After a quick stop at the McDonald's drive-thru for some Egg McMuffins and grease sponges—a.k.a. hash browns —Stone headed out of town toward Lake Clear.

Holly owned a small, simple, two-story house with detached garage perched on a two-acre parcel a few miles past the Adirondack Regional Airport. Surrounded by pine trees and the nearest neighbor a good half-mile up the road, the homestead offered peace and privacy. Stone knew that Holly was a woman with secrets, so he wasn't surprised that she lived out here, away from the gossip and rumor-mongering of town.

The road rounded a bend and then straightened before reaching Holly's house. As he steered the Blazer out of the curve, Stone spotted a truck parked across the road from the driveway. The hazard lights flashed in one-second orange winks.

Innocent enough at first glance; a broke-down traveler with car trouble who'd pulled off the side of the road while they waited for a tow truck. Nothing to be alarmed about. Route 30 was a back-country road, but it served as a primary connector between Saranac Lake and Tupper Lake, and as such, saw its fair share of travelers.

Still, something about the vehicle on the side of the road raised Stone's hackles. All those years spent on the killing fields had honed a razor edge on his survival instincts. Some of that sharpness may have dulled since he traded his blasters for a Bible, but his sense of danger still operated at a higher level than most. And right now, those senses warned him there was something wrong about that hazard-flashing truck.

As he drove closer, Stone saw that it was a Dodge Ram pickup truck. Green, splattered with mud. Could be swamp mud, could be mud from the road...no way to tell.

He drove past the Dodge. He couldn't see anyone in the cab. He glanced the other way and caught a glimpse of a jacked-up Jeep Wrangler parked in Holly's driveway, next to her flat-tired Gladiator.

What the hell?

He kept driving and in his rearview mirror he saw the silhouette of someone sitting up in the Dodge Ram. They must have been slumped down in the cab to make it look like the truck was abandoned while he passed by.

Stone growled a curse. He knew that wasn't a good sign.

He also intended to do something about it.

He turned onto Dump Road. If the occupant in the Dodge was watching him in their rearview mirror, hopefully they would assume Stone was heading to the Lake Clear Transfer Station to dump some garbage.

He drove a short distance up the road and then pulled the Chevy onto the shoulder, snow and gravel crunching under the tires. He double-checked his Colt revolver to make sure all six chambers bristled with brass, then put the pistol back in his coat pocket.

"Stay here, boy," he said to Max. "I'll be back."

The dog gave him a look that said, *Take your time. I've got all day.*

Stone climbed the snowbank that edged the road and entered the tree-line. The pines weren't as thick as they were on his property back in Whisper Falls, but the snow-burdened boughs drooped low, making for hard going. Dislodged snow drifted down and bounced off his Stetson as he trudged through the woods back toward Route 30.

He crossed the road in a rush, praying that the whoever was in the Dodge wouldn't choose that moment to check their rearview mirror and spot Stone sneaking into the woods. If that happened, his stealth approach would be blown, and he would resort to a more direct confrontation.

He waited inside the woods for a few minutes to see if the Ram sped away, but it just sat there, flashers blinking.

Moving parallel to the road, Stone maneuvered through the trees toward the truck. The trees thinned out here, but still clustered together enough to camouflage his approach. He moved slowly, cautiously, fully aware that fast motion attracted the human eye. He was in sneak-and-peek reconnaissance mode; right now he just wanted to see who was in the Dodge. Once he possessed that information, he would decide what to do next. If it was just an innocent motorist stranded on the side of the road, he would offer to help. But if it was some kind of threat…

Well, that would be a whole other story.

Stone emerged from the tree-line behind and to the right of the Ram, out of view of the rearview mirror. He ducked low as he approached the back bumper, the metal cold beneath his bare fingers. He'd left his gloves in the Blazer, not wanting them to slow his draw if he had to go for the gun quickly. His hands were cold and ruddy from exposure, but he'd suffered worse. He tried not to think about that mission in Antarctica. He'd never known frostbite could hurt so badly.

Peering around the truck's tailgate, Stone saw that he had caught a lucky break. A thin sheen of ice frosted over the passenger-side mirror, rendering the glass opaque. Either the Dodge featured no mirror defrosters, or the driver had been too lazy to scrape it off. Whatever the reason, it made Stone's approach a whole lot easier.

Staying low, he crept along the side of the truck until he crouched just below the passenger-side window. He slid his hand into his pocket, cold fingers curling around the Colt Cobra's grips. He then slowly raised his head like a periscope breaching the water's surface and looked inside the cab.

The first thing he saw was the back of a man's head, looking away from him, staring across the road at Holly's house. A pair of binoculars rested on the dashboard, proving the guy had been playing peeping tom. Stone could hear the faint strains of music turned down low, the stereo playing some pop-country cover of a Christmas carol to pass the time on the stakeout.

The second thing he saw was a matte black Taurus TH40 semi-automatic, fitted with a sound suppressor, lying on the middle console.

TWENTY-ONE

STONE GRITTED HIS TEETH. Yeah, this wasn't some innocent tourist with car trouble.

The driver's left arm was stretched out, resting along the window. A cast peeked out from the cuff of his camouflage jacket, bright white in contrast to the muted browns, blacks, and greens. The cast looked fresh.

Stone didn't waste any more time. He knew what needed to be done.

His eyes flicked downward. The truck doors were locked.

No problem.

He pulled the .38 from his pocket, rose quickly while the driver still faced the opposite direction, and used the barrel to smash open the passenger-side window. Shattered glass tumbled into the cab.

The driver jerked, caught off-guard, but recovered quickly. His right hand reached for the Taurus.

But Stone already had him dead to rights.

He thrust the .38 through the busted window and shoved it into the man's face. "Touch that gun and I'll turn your ugly mug into dog food," he rasped.

The driver—the man he had dubbed Blackbeard during the bar brawl—looked pissed, but complied, pulling his hand back and letting it rest on the steering wheel.

"Unlock the door."

Blackbeard moved his left arm, tapping a button on his door console with his index finger. The lock popped up with a mechanical *thunk*.

Stone climbed into the cab and slammed the door shut behind him. He rammed the muzzle of the Colt Cobra under the man's jaw, tilting his head upward and pinning it against the window. "Remember me? Or do I need to break your other wrist to remind you?"

"Yeah, I know who you are," Blackbeard grunted. "I never forget an asshole."

Keeping the .38 tight against the survivalist's face, Stone snatched up the man's Taurus with his left hand. If he needed to use a gun, he preferred to use one with a suppressor. The nearest neighbor might be a half-mile away, but the roar of a .38—even inside the truck — would be plenty loud enough to be heard. A suppressed .40 caliber, however, would sound like nothing more than a dropped phonebook. You'd barely hear it fifty meters away.

If he decided to shoot this son of a bitch, the fewer people that knew about it, the better.

"What are you doing here?" Stone asked.

Blackbeard didn't say anything.

"Silence is not an option." Stone rested the Taurus on the man's thigh, muzzle angled down so that the end of the suppressor grazed his zipper. "Unless you're looking for a sex change."

"Good God!" Blackbeard exclaimed. "What kind of preacher threatens to blow a man's balls off?"

"The kind that's really ticked off that a scumbag like

you is hanging around the house of people he cares about." Stone shoved hard with the Taurus. "Start talking."

The survivalist yelped and tried to recoil as the pistol threatened to crush his manhood. "All right! All right! Relax, will ya?" Nervous sweat beaded on his temples and trickled down to vanish into the bristly thicket of his beard. "Carl sent me over here."

"Why?"

"You know why."

"Tell me anyway."

"You killed four of our guys last night!"

"They came at me. I put them down. Nothing more to it."

"Carl don't see it like that," Blackbeard replied. "You killed some of his boys and blood demands blood."

"Holly and Lizzy had nothing to do with those men getting killed last night."

"Sometimes revenge has collateral damage."

Stone almost shot him right then and there but managed to resist temptation. "Whose Jeep in the driveway?" he asked.

Blackbeard shrugged. "Not sure. Some jock-wannabe punk. Showed up after Holly went to work."

"If Holly's at work and Lizzy's at school, why are you watching the house?"

"Lizzy ain't at school."

"What are you talking about?"

"She's still in the house. Sick or playing hooky or something like that." His unkempt beard split open in a deranged, lascivious grin. "Probably getting banged real good by jock boy."

Stone needed to get inside the house. No more time to waste on this jackass. "Thanks for the info," he said. "You've been very helpful."

"So you're gonna let me live, right?"

"Yeah, you get to live," Stone replied. "But I want you to deliver a message to Carl for me."

"Sure, no problem. What is it?"

Stone shifted the Taurus' aim and shot him in the left leg.

The suppressed gunshot eclipsed the wet smack of the bullet tearing through the tender flesh of his inner thigh at a downward angle, just missing the bone to bury itself in the seat.

Blackbeard let out an agonized howl.

Stone ground the muzzle of the Colt Cobra into the survivalist's chin. "Shut up or I'll blow your lower jaw off and you'll have to sign-language the damn message when you get back to Carl."

Blackbeard didn't go completely silent—probably in too much pain for that—but he did manage to dial it back to a whimper. His eyes bugged out of his head as he looked sideways over the Colt's muzzle at the pissed-off preacher.

"The message is this," Stone growled. "You tell Carl that anyone messes with me or the people I care for, I'll kill every one of you sons of bitches, right down to the last man."

Blackbeard's apoplectic eyes were black circles rimmed by bloodshot whites, burning with a boiling cocktail of pain, hate, and fear. He shivered and the vibrations traveled through the cold steel of the .38 to Stone's firm, unwavering hand.

"You got that?" Stone asked.

"Yeah," Blackbeard hissed through pain-clenched teeth. "I got it."

"Good." Stone exited the truck.

Outside, the winter air bit into him again, but the adrenalin pumping through his bloodstream kept the cold at bay. He dropped the Colt back into his coat pocket and ejected the magazine from the Taurus. He thumb-flicked the rounds out, dropping them into the icy slush on the side of the road. He then tossed the empty magazine into the woods, followed by the gun itself. They disappeared into the snow drifts. With his broken wrist and wounded leg, there was no way Blackbeard would be able to retrieve them.

Stone glared through the broken window. "Go on, get out of here. That leg needs fixing and that message isn't going to deliver itself."

"You're a dead man," Blackbeard warned. "You're a ghost who don't even know it yet."

"People keep telling me that," Stone replied. "But here I am, still alive and kicking."

With a final scowl, Blackbeard shifted into gear and peeled out onto the road, heading back toward Sinkhole Hollow Swamp. He gunned the gas as he departed, the rear wheels of the truck spitting icy gravel and slushy snow in twin rooster-tails that peppered Stone's pants. A vehicular "fuck you" if ever there was one.

Stone ignored it. He'd broken Blackbeard's wrist and put a bullet in his leg. As "fuck yous" went, that trumped road-spray any day of the week and twice on Sundays.

As the Dodge faded into the distance, he dashed across the road. With no neighbors, he didn't need to be furtive or discreet. He just went up to the house and started looking in the windows. He didn't want to knock on the door and reveal his presence until he knew what was going on inside, even though he already had a strong suspicion.

There was a screened porch attached to the front of the house. The shoveled path revealed a narrow flagstone walkway. He moved quickly but cautiously, not wanting to slip on the icy stones.

The porch door opened with a low, rusty creak, but Stone doubted the house occupants were paying any attention. He crept forward and pressed himself against the wall outside the window that looked into the living room. The curtains were drawn, but there was just enough of a gap for him to see through.

Lizzy laid on the couch, deep-kissing the older teenage guy—Michael, he assumed—on top of her. Her state of undress pissed Stone off. Michael's roaming hands pissed him off even more.

They hadn't bothered to lock the door and Stone didn't bother knocking.

TWENTY-TWO

LIZZY YELPED as Stone barged into the room. She scrambled to push Michael away and yank her blouse closed. "Luke!" she yelled. "What the hell?"

"Hey, Lizzy." Stone kept his voice deceptively calm to mask his anger. "Your mom asked me to stop by and fix her tire. I thought you'd be in school."

"I skipped. Wasn't feeling well." Her excuse sounded caught somewhere between shame and defiance.

"Yeah, being molested by a punk will do that to you sometimes."

By now, Michael had managed to stand up. He wasn't wearing a shirt, exposing linebacker shoulders and the kind of thick chest muscles that come from the benefit of youth and countless hours in the gym. He still had his pants on, but his belt hung open, a large brass buckle shaped like a football helmet dangling from the leather strap.

"Who the hell are you?" he demanded.

Lizzy answered. "His name's Stone. Or Luke. He's my mom's new boyfriend, or friend, or whatever they are."

"If Stone or Luke don't suit you," Stone said, "you can just call me preacher."

"Preacher, huh? Well, *preacher*, what the hell are you doing here?"

"Came to tell you about Jesus." Stone's voice became cold as a winter grave. "Because next time you put your hands on Lizzy, you're gonna meet Him."

"Oh, for the love of God, Luke…" Lizzy groaned.

"Nice speech, preacher," Michael mocked. "But now it's time for you to go. So either drag your shit-talking ass out of here or I'll throw it out for you." He added with a smirk, "Or maybe you want to sit down and watch the show while I give Lizzy a good time."

Stone knew there was a verse in the Bible—Ecclesiastes 3:1—that stated there was a time for everything, and right now it was time to take this smug player down a couple notches.

"Michael," he said with a smile that never reached his eyes, "you seem like such a nice kid, so it's a real shame that I'm going to beat the crap out of you."

"Bring it, preacher-man."

Stone brought it.

He closed the gap between him and Michael in four long strides, dodged the amateur haymaker the teenager launched at him, and fired a short, powerful blow to the guy's solar plexus. Not hard enough to put him down for good, but more than enough to blast the wind out of his sails and wrench a gasp of pain from his lips.

"Luke!" Lizzy yelled. "Leave him alone!"

Stone ignored her as Michael recovered enough to launch another punch, a wicked uppercut aimed at his chin. Stone blocked the blow and countered with a right cross that caught the teenager flush on the face. The punishing impact of rough knuckles striking jawbone sent Michael staggering sideways. He hit the couch, lost his balance, and tumbled over the back, hitting the floor with a loud thump.

Stone circled around behind the couch as Michael climbed to his feet. Stone grabbed a fistful of the teenager's hair and yanked his head back. Michael's breath wheezed out of him from the solar plexus strike and his left jaw glowed red from the recent blow.

"You listening to me yet?" Stone rasped. "Or do I need to beat it into you some more?"

"You can't do this," Michael croaked. "You'll go to jail for assaulting a high school student."

"You're eighteen," Stone replied. "And that makes you an adult. An adult caught in the act of trying to commit statutory rape." He smiled mirthlessly. "This isn't an assault, Michael. It's a citizen's arrest. And since you're resisting, I'm authorized to use whatever force is necessary to take you into custody."

"Just let me go."

"I don't know about that. I'm a big fan of beating on dirtbags who prey on young girls."

"Come on, man. Let me go. I'll leave her alone, I swear."

"Michael!" Lizzy said. "What the hell's that about? You said we have something special. Now you're just going to give it all up?"

Michael didn't even look at her. Just kept his eyes fixed on Stone. "Sorry, Liz, but you ain't worth taking a beat-down for. I can get a piece of ass anywhere."

"You jerk!" she screamed, face flushing red with shame and rage.

Stone threw the guy against the wall so hard that he cracked the sheetrock, ricocheted off, and fell to his knees. He stayed there, looking up at Stone, smart enough to know when he was outclassed in a fight.

"Get up and get out of here," Stone growled. "You come around Lizzy again, I'll put you in the hospital."

"You're not calling the cops?"

"You're not just a scumbag, you're a stupid scumbag." Stone sighed heavily, making it clear that his patience was wearing thin. "If you're not gone in about three seconds, I'm going to start breaking bones. You need me to count it down for you?"

Michael made it out the door with his shirt missing and his belt still unbuckled in just under five seconds, but Stone figured that was close enough. About ten seconds later the Jeep fired up and Michael hit the road. Probably cold as hell without a shirt or jacket, but Stone didn't give a damn.

He walked back around to the front of the couch and found Lizzy huddled up in the corner, arms crossed defiantly as she glared at him. "Happy now?" she snapped. "You got to play the knight in shining armor who rushed to my rescue before that wicked boy could rob me of my virtue."

"Like I said," Stone replied, "I just came over to fix your mother's flat tire. But I'm glad I got here in time to keep you from making a mistake."

"I'll just make the mistake some other time."

"Sure you will, but you might want to give it another couple of years."

She rolled her eyes so hard that Stone figured she must have seen the back of her skull. "Give me a break, Luke. Fifteen is plenty old enough to have sex."

Stone knew he was out of his element here, chatting with a 15-year-old girl about when to lose her virginity. But clearly someone needed to talk to her about it and he was the only one around right now. "Fifteen is still a little young," he said. "I think the average for a girl is somewhere around seventeen, last I heard."

"If that's the average, then that means fifty percent of girls are under seventeen," Lizzy countered. "So it's not like I'm way out in left field here, Luke."

She was a smart kid, Stone had to give her that. "Listen," he said, "I get it. I was a teenager once too, not so long ago."

"Yeah? And how old were you when you did it for the first time?"

"Older than you'd think, but it was still a mistake."

His confession pierced through her fog of defiance and grabbed her attention. She tilted her head quizzically. "What do you mean?" No rough edge to her voice; she sounded like she sincerely wanted to know.

"I didn't love her," Stone said. "She was older, stuck in a bad marriage, and just looking for a younger guy to make her feel better. We hooked up one afternoon and we both got to live with the guilt and regret for a long time afterwards."

"That's different," Lizzy argued. "She was married. That's why it was wrong for you to be with her."

"Even if she'd been single, it still would've been wrong, because there was no love involved." Stone paused a moment to let that sink in, then pressed on. "Listen, Lizzy, I'm not one of those no-sex-before-marriage preachers."

"Shocking," she drawled sarcastically. "You're usually so traditional in your beliefs."

"But I do believe that sex should be with someone you love, not just a physical 'wham-bam' hookup."

"Says the guy who just admitted he hooked up."

"Says the guy who also just told you he regrets it."

"Regret comes from mistakes and those mistakes teach us lessons," Lizzy said. "You can tell me all about your mistakes and regrets, Luke, but at some point, I'm going to have to make my own mistakes, live with my own regrets, and learn my own lessons."

"You're right," Stone said. "But that doesn't mean you need to be in a rush to be stupid."

"Like today? That what you're getting at?"

"I think Michael made it pretty clear you're nothing special to him."

"Yeah." She looked crestfallen, clearly having suffered a blow to the heart. "He turned out to be a total jerk."

"Asshole."

"What?"

"Guy like that is far beyond your regular, run-of-the-mill jerk," Stone said. "He's a total asshole."

Lizzy laughed. "You're either the best preacher in the world, or the worst, but thanks for the pep talk."

"Just don't want to see you go down a bad road. You're a good kid, Lizzy, with a good head on your shoulders."

"Well, gee, thanks so much, *padre*." She flipped her purple-streaked hair in an exaggerated, shampoo-commercial motion. "I thought you'd never notice."

The corner of Stone's lips tugged up in a smile. He liked this girl. He needed to be careful not to make her a surrogate for the daughter he had lost. She deserved better than to just be a stand-in for his hurting heart.

Lizzy suddenly frowned. "Um, Luke? What about mom?"

"What about her?"

"Are you…" Her voice trailed off and she fidgeted for a few seconds before heaving a huge, *let's-just-get-this-over-with* sigh and asking, "Are you gonna tell her about this?"

Stone nodded without hesitation. "I have to."

"Actually, no, you don't. It can be our little secret. You know, like smoking a cigarette the other night."

"Not telling your mom that you snuck a cigarette is one thing. Not telling her that you skipped school to get it on with an eighteen-year-old is another."

"Come on, Luke! Cut me some slack here!"

"Absolutely not. She has a right to know."

Lizzy looked miserable. "Well, can you at least let *me* tell her?"

"Sure." He nodded. "That's actually a good idea, own up to your mistake. Shows maturity."

"She's still gonna ground the crap out of me."

Stone grinned. "You bet she is. But you'll live."

"Fine, I'll tell her when she gets home."

"I hope so," he replied. "Because I'm coming back for dinner tonight and if you haven't told her by then, I will."

"Well, isn't that just freaking great." She groaned, threw her head back against the sofa, and rolled her eyes at the ceiling to express her disbelief at her rotten luck.

Stone chuckled and said, "See ya later, Lizzy," and then headed outside to fix Holly's flat.

He was tightening the last lug on the spare tire when his cell phone started vibrating, still silenced from when he had turned it off to sneak up on Blackbeard. He put down the wrench, fished the phone from his pocket, and saw that it was Holly calling.

"Hey," he answered. "I'm just finishing up with your truck."

"Luke." Her voice crackled with a brittle, panicked edge. "I just got a call from the school. Holly didn't show up today."

"I know," he said, keeping his own tone calm and reassuring. "She's here at the house."

"What? Why?"

"Skipping school, it would seem," Stone said, keeping

it simple. He had promised to give Lizzy a chance to come clean and he would keep that promise.

"Skipping? Oh, she is *so* grounded."

"Oh, I've got no doubt about that," Stone said, silently adding, *You don't know the half of it.*

"But she's safe? You're sure about that?"

"I'm sure." Stone heard something in Holly's voice, something that ran deeper than the normal alarm a mother would feel about not knowing where their daughter was.

Holly sighed long and heavy on the other end, releasing her pent-up anxiety. "Thank God for that, at least."

"Holly, is there something you want to tell me?"

A long pause, then: "Uh, what do you mean?"

Stone frowned and shook his head, even though she couldn't see him. "Nothing. Forget I asked. You just seem a little off."

"You don't know what it's like to have a daughter to worry about all the time."

Stone winced. That one stung.

Holly instantly realized her faux pas. "Oh my God, Luke! I am so sorry! I didn't mean…" She sounded utterly horrified as her voice trailed off.

She clearly hadn't meant to hurt him and Stone let her off the hook easy. "It's okay. You're upset and that just came out wrong."

"I'm so, so sorry."

"Stop apologizing," he said. "It was an honest mistake."

"More like a boneheaded mistake."

"All right, I'll give you that one," he replied. "It *was* a pretty boneheaded thing to say." He kept his tone light and easy to make sure she knew everything was fine between them.

"Dinner tonight," she said. "I'll make it up to you."

"Just don't overcook my Raman noodles and we'll call it even."

They said their goodbyes and hung up. Stone finished up with the tire and went back inside to say goodbye to Lizzy, but she was in the shower belting out a classic Bon Jovi tune at the top of her lungs while steam rolled out from under the door. He grinned to himself as he left the house. The kid might have made some bad choices today, but at least she had good taste in music.

Max was asleep when Stone got back to the truck, curled up in a ball on the seat of the Blazer like a puppy instead of the 110 lb. beast he was. The Shottie lifted his head as Stone slid into the driver's seat and gave him a look that said, *Took you long enough, man. All good?*

Stone started the engine, then reached over and scratched the dog between the ears. He wondered if Blackbeard had made it back to the swamp with his message yet. "There are some bad people in this town, Max, and I'm not sure what to do about that."

He moved his hand away to crank up the heat and Max settled back down without offering any answers.

Still, as he drove down the road, headed back to the church, a canine analogy crept into Stone's mind.

Sometimes you just bark at trouble, but sometimes you have to bite.

Stone was starting to think that maybe it was time to show his teeth.

TWENTY-THREE

WHEN STONE RETURNED to the Bennet residence shortly before six o'clock that night, Lizzy was nowhere to be found.

"Where's Lizzy?" he asked. He had brought a bottle of wine that he now set down on the dining room table.

"In her room." Holly stood at the counter, piling cold cuts onto hoagie rolls. Apparently, she had not been joking about serving him a sandwich for supper. "She'll be lucky if I let her out before New Year's Eve."

"Guess that means she 'fessed up."

"Yes, she told me."

Holly had loosened her hair from its usual ponytail, letting it fall free. Her jeans did a nice job of hugging her hips without veering into too-tight territory while a sky-blue blouse did the same to her upper curves.

On her feet, she wore bright blue bunny slippers.

"I like your shoes," Stone said with a teasing grin.

She looked down, shook her head in self-deprecating disbelief, and said, "What can I say? The floor is cold and I meant to change them before you showed up, but then I got sidetracked by all the Lizzy drama."

"No problem. You're in your house, not down at the Jack Lumber."

"I can take them off."

"No need. They're cute." He winked at her. "Kind of like the person wearing them."

She smiled as she brought over the sandwiches and set them on the table. "Well, look who showed up with an extra helping of charm tonight."

"And wine."

"Not sure wine goes with sandwiches, but what the heck."

She took a plate up to Lizzy's room while Stone poured two glasses of Pinot Noir. He wasn't much of a wine drinker, but he could tolerate it enough to be sociable. Besides, letting her drink alone just seemed ungentlemanly, and when he finished telling her everything, she was definitely going to need the alcohol.

When she came back, Stone let her get three bites into her turkey sandwich before he started filling her in on recent events, beginning with the attack at his house the night before and ending with his confrontation with Blackbeard this morning. She was easy to talk to and he spared nothing, giving her the raw, unvarnished truth.

She listened without interruption, though she looked worried as he recounted the violence of the assassination attempt. Then she chewed slowly, thoughtfully, as he relayed his conversations with Sheriff Camden and Deacon White.

But worry turned to outright alarm when he told her about Blackbeard staking out her house. Her face paled and she swallowed hard, as if her bite of sandwich had just solidified into a large lump of clay.

"So Lizzy and I are in danger." She phrased it as a statement, not a question.

Stone opted for honesty rather than comfort. "Looks that way," he replied. "But it's me they really want."

She looked at him with some of the saddest eyes he had ever seen and he realized they were welling up with tears, giving the brilliant blue a fragile sheen. "Luke," she said softly, "you should go."

Her words caught him off guard. "You want me to leave?"

She nodded. "Yes." Then she shook her head. "No." Finally, she let out a burdened sigh. "I mean, no, I don't *want* you to go, but I think you should."

He leaned back in his chair, feeling a bit stunned. "I'll hit the road if that's what you want, but do you mind telling me why?"

"Because Lizzy and I have to leave."

"What do you mean?"

"We have to leave here." Holly waved her hand in a vague gesture.

"This house?"

She looked miserable. "This house. This town. Probably this state."

"Because of the swamp rats?"

"Because we're in danger, and when we're in danger, we have to move." She stared down at her sandwich as if contained the answers to the mysteries of the world. "There's really no choice." When she lifted her head, a tear escaped each eye, trickling down her face in twin streaks of sadness. "I'll probably never see you again and I suck at goodbyes, so I think it would be best if you just got up and walked out that door without saying anything."

Stone leaned forward in his chair, pushed aside his sandwich, folded his hands on the table in front of him, and said, "No."

Holly blinked, surprised. "What?"

"I'm not leaving until you tell me what's going on."

"I can't," she said miserably.

"Then I guess I'll be sitting here awhile."

Neither of them said anything for the next few minutes. It was so quiet, Stone could hear the clock on the wall behind him, each tick carving away a sliver of time. Holly looked down at her hands and fidgeted, but apparently couldn't bring herself to speak.

Stone just sat there and waited her out. He would sit here all night if that's what it took.

Finally, she looked up and studied his face with a piercing, focused gaze before she broke the silence with a question. "Can I trust you, Luke?"

Stone almost reached across the table and took her hand but decided against it. "Of course you can."

"I mean, really, *really* trust you," she said. "Like, trust you with my life. Because that's what you're asking me to do."

He locked eyes with her. "You can trust me with your life, I promise."

She nodded, bit her lower lip for a moment, and then blurted out her secret. "Lizzy and I are in the Witness Protection Program."

TWENTY-FOUR

AS SECRETS WENT, that one was a whopper, and it let Stone know just how much Holly trusted him. Telling him the truth meant he could betray her, sell her out, endanger her and Lizzy. She truly had put her life in his hands. He felt even more drawn to her, like a bond deepening.

"The Witness Security Program," Stone said, referring to it by its technical name. He'd worked with a WITSEC team once in the aftermath of a mission, when a high-value target turned against a genocidal warlord and had needed to disappear after giving his testimony. Stone had found the U.S. Marshals to be highly skilled and efficient at their jobs. As far as he knew, the turncoat witness was still living a comfortable life as a gentleman farmer on a Wyoming ranch, courtesy of the U.S. taxpayers.

She nodded. "Right. WITSEC. We've been in the program for the past eight years."

"That's why you're in Whisper Falls. The Marshals set you up here with a new life, new identities."

She nodded again.

Now Stone understood why she had been reluctant to

talk about her past beyond the most basic of details, and even those scant details had probably been fabricated. It also explained why she had been so worried when Holly missed school yesterday. WITSEC wasn't perfect and sometimes the bad guys found their prey. As a mother, she had feared the worst.

"Can you tell me why?"

"I'll tell you everything," she said. "I've made some bad decisions in my life, but I don't think trusting you is one of them."

She began by telling him her and Lizzy's real names, which Stone immediately did his best to forget. He didn't want to think of them as anyone else. To him, they would always be Holly and Lizzy.

She kept the tragic tale relatively short and definitely not sweet, glossing over the fine print to give him just the bare-bones facts. No doubt she would fill in the blanks later if he asked, but right now she seemed like she just wanted to get the story told, as if there was some catharsis to be found by finally sharing her secrets with someone.

———

She ran a low-stakes blackjack table at an off-strip casino in Nevada. It was common knowledge that the west coast mafia owned and operated the place, but for Holly, it was just a job. She came to work, pulled her shift, and went home.

That all changed the night Jack 'Lucky Draw' Dawson rolled into town.

Notorious for his skill at Texas Hold 'Em—which had earned him his nickname—Dawson dressed like an Old West gambler, fancily fashioned in black jeans, white shirt, maroon vest, and a black Stetson sporting a band that matched the dark purple of his vest. Even his black cowboy boots boasted a pattern stitched with maroon thread. Black and blood-red, those were Dawson's colors.

It would have looked ridiculous on anyone else, but Dawson somehow pulled it off, and when his sparkling green eyes glanced Holly's way, she felt his magnetism seducing her. He treated her to a crooked smile that was both charming and edged with wickedness, the kind of smile that let her know that yeah, he was a bit of a bad boy, but he was a good bad boy.

She didn't believe in love at first sight—that was for twittering schoolgirls who hadn't been roughed up by life yet—but an immediate attraction definitely flared between them. When he moved away—surrounded by what seemed like a posse of stern-looking men—she somehow knew that she would be seeing him again.

He was waiting for her at the end of her shift, effortlessly steering her to the bar for a drink that soon turned into many drinks. Then he revealed that he owned the casino. Fogged up with alcohol, her inebriated brain didn't make the connection that he was a mob boss.

They spent the night together in a torrid fling, neither of them believing it would be anything more than a one-night stand. No love, just hot lust. A young woman who hadn't felt passion about anything or anyone for a long time and a Las Vegas crime lord accustomed to taking whatever he wanted.

Their lovemaking was unbridled, raw, and rough. She didn't realize just how rough until she woke up in the morning to find him gone but her body blotched with bruises. Looking back, she should have seen it as a warning sign, but that morning, she just chalked it up to drunken sex that had gotten a little out of control. Besides, she never expected to see him again.

A pregnancy test two months later proved that wrong.

He played the gentleman and married her—after she signed a pre-nuptial agreement that guaranteed she wouldn't get more *than a pittance in a divorce—and soon thereafter Lizzy was born.*

Things were fine for the first several years. It wasn't a true marriage—Dawson continued to go out and screw any pretty young thing that caught his eye—but they all got along fine and maintained the semblance of being a family. Despite his infidelity, Dawson made sure his wife and daughter wanted for nothing.

During those "happy" years, Holly got a glimpse behind the curtain and learned about the criminal empire her husband ruled over. She learned about the dirty tricks the casino used to tip the odds even more in the house's favor. She learned about the prostitution ring running out of the back of the place. She learned about the narcotics and pharmaceuticals being sold behind one of the bars. She learned which politicians were on the take. She even learned where a couple of bodies were buried.

She tucked away all the knowledge and kept her mouth shut. Partly because she enjoyed the life of luxury provided to her and Lizzy, but mostly because she didn't want to end up as one of those corpses buried out in the desert or picked clean by the buzzards. Dawson only tolerated her because she was low maintenance. The moment she became a burden, he would scrub her from his life. Afraid of what would happen to Lizzy if she was murdered, Holly kept her eyes open but her mouth shut.

That didn't change when Dawson became abusive. She never knew why he started hitting her, the reasons behind his sudden outbursts of violence. Maybe his business endeavors were taking a hit. Maybe he had lost favor with his criminal overlords. Maybe there was an erupting brain tumor that had flicked some sort of caveman switch in his cerebral cortex.

The reasons didn't matter when her skin split beneath his angry knuckles, when her flesh swelled and bruised and reddened from his raging blows. Black eyes, cracked ribs, twisted limbs...she suffered it all with tears and silence. Not because she believed she deserved it—she was not one of those broken, self-loathing women who think they have it coming—but because this was Lizzy's home, her life. She had nowhere else to go and besides, even if she left, Dawson would hunt her down and have her killed.

No, she decided, she would do anything for her daughter, including suffer punishment at the hands of an abusive husband. The blood and bruises were the sacrifice, the price she paid to keep Lizzy from a life on the run, always looking over their shoulder, wondering when the bullet would come screaming out of the night to scramble her skull.

But everything changed the night Dawson beat Lizzy for the first time.

Holly was asleep in her bed, not hearing the sounds of Dawson coming home from whatever nocturnal activities had kept him out on the town until the witching hour. But she woke up when Lizzy's terrified screams fractured the quiet.

She leaped out of bed and raced down the hall to Lizzy's room as if the hounds of hell were snapping at her bare heels.

She threw open the door so hard that it bounced off the wall. On the four-poster bed with purple sheets emblazoned with yellow ponies, Dawson straddled his five-year-old daughter, slapping her face viciously. Blood streamed from Lizzy's nostrils and her sleep-crusted eyes were already starting to swell shut. She sobbed and cried out, "Please, Daddy, stop!"

"You little bitch!" Dawson snarled. "I'll teach you to tell me no!"

The sound of his fists hitting their little girl was something Holly would never forget. She threw herself across the room and attacked him with all the primal ferocity of a mother bear protecting her cub.

She pulled his hair and raked his face with her nails, clawing for his eyes but missing, peeling away strips of skin from his cheeks in red, blood-welling ruts. She pounded clenched fists against the back of his neck, trying to shatter the top of his spine. She thudded her knees into his ribs, hoping to snap a bone and drive it into his lungs.

She turned herself into a frantic, flailing, violent dervish of maternal fury. All she wanted to do was kill him for daring to hurt their daughter.

Instead, he almost killed her.

He fended off her blind-rage blows. A hard right hook to the temple sent her reeling to the floor where he pounced on her like a pissed-off badger. The kicks and punches meant for Lizzy now pounded against her face, her body, her legs. She welcomed them. He could beat her until dawn cracked the sky as long as it meant he wasn't beating Lizzy.

Somewhere beyond the crimson blur of pain, she heard Lizzy screaming. She fought to stay conscious for as long as possible, but the human body can only take so much torment. By the time her second cheekbone cracked beneath her crushed and flattened nose, she blacked out.

She came around to find Dawson gone and a hysterical Lizzy shaking her back to agonizing life. Blood spattered the carpet in all directions, an abstract pattern of pain and misery. But other than the initial beating, Lizzy was untouched, so Holly's sacrifice had been more than worth it.

By the time morning came, she was lying in a hospital bed, bruises salved, skin stitched, wounds bandaged, broken bones set. They offered her pain medication but she refused. She knew what she needed to do and didn't want her brain operating in an anesthetic haze when she did it.

She called the FBI.

Agents swarmed her room in less than an hour. Before the day ended, she cut a deal to spill her guts about Jack 'Lucky Draw' Dawson's criminal empire, to confess all the sins and secrets she knew in exchange for a new life far away from Las Vegas. She didn't care where. The only thing that mattered was that she and Lizzy would be safe.

———

"I testified at the trial and Jack ended up getting twenty-five to life," Holly said. "They threw the book at him, using all the information I gave them."

"Where is he now?" Stone asked.

"Last I knew, rotting in Lompoc federal prison."

"Does Lizzy know the whole story?"

"Most of it." Holly's eyes were haunted, still trapped somewhere in the darkness of her past. "That son of a bitch made a big mistake when he decided to put his hands on my baby girl."

"Sounds like he got what was coming to him, thanks to you."

"Yeah, he can rot in hell, for all I care. I'll do whatever it takes to protect Lizzy." She looked at Stone. "Which is why we have to leave."

"You don't really think the survivalists are connected to your ex-husband, do you?"

"Doesn't matter," she replied. "Anytime I'm in danger, the feds move me. All part of the deal. Once I tell my WITSEC handlers about this, they'll get me and Lizzy out of here ASAP."

"Don't call them."

"Luke, I have to. For Lizzy's sake. I told you, I'll do anything to protect her. I can't stay here if Carl and his pack of trigger-happy assholes have made us targets."

"I'll take care of it."

He spoke the five words with such force that she sat back in her chair as if struck by a powerful wind. She studied his face as she asked, "What are you going to do?"

"Whatever it takes," he replied grimly, then pushed back his chair and stood up. "I'm gonna say goodbye to Lizzy and then head out."

"You haven't even finished your sandwich."

"I've got things to do," he said. "When I'm gone, lock the doors and don't open them until you hear from me. You still have that pistol?"

Holly nodded. "It's in my purse."

"Get it out and keep it with you. Any of the swamp rats show their faces, put a bullet in them. Hell, make it three bullets, just to be sure they're good and dead."

"Sure, why not?" Holly said. "A murder charge will look great on my resume."

"Any of those assholes show up here and you put them down, I promise you there won't be any murder charges."

"How can you be so sure?"

"Because I know people that will make sure that doesn't happen," he said.

Holly stood up and walked around the table until she was right in front of him. Her blue eyes searched his face as if trying to decipher his secrets. Stone felt drawn to her as both a friend and something more, something that probably wasn't best for either of them right now.

"Who are you?" she asked quietly.

"I'm just a guy trying to help some people he cares about," he replied.

She moved closer. He could feel her warmth. She said, "You're a good man, Luke Stone," and then raised up on her tiptoes in her bunny slippers.

For one brief heartbeat, he thought she was going to kiss him on the mouth. But before he could even decide how to respond, she dodged left, and her lips fell gently on his cheek. He felt disappointed and relieved in equal measure.

Despite his better judgement, he folded her into his arms in a tight, comforting embrace. She melted against him, face buried against his chest. Her arms slid around his waist, holding him close.

They didn't linger in the moment, both of them sensing that the closeness would become something more if they weren't careful.

Holly stepped back and reluctantly, Stone let her go. Not wanting awkward silence to ruin the moment they had just shared, he said, "I'm gonna go say goodbye to Lizzy."

He took the stairs up to the second floor. Lizzy's room was at the far end of the hallway. As he headed that way, Stone noticed the peeling paint and warped molding. WITSEC certainly hadn't relocated them to a lavish life. But maybe that was the point. Nobody would look for an ex-mob wife working as a waitress while living in a rundown house in one of the coldest parts of the country.

Holly's door was open. She sat Indian-style on her bed, reading a novel. She looked up as Stone's large frame filled the doorway.

"So," she said, setting the book down. "You happy? You got me grounded."

"Pretty sure you got yourself grounded," he replied. "But nice try at deflecting guilt."

"Mom was royally pissed."

"She had a right to be."

Lizzy brushed a few strands of purple hair from her eyes. "So I guess you know all our dirty little secrets now." Without waiting for him to respond, she said, "I heard mom telling you everything. Sound travels right up those stairs and down this hall a whole lot better than people think."

"Does it bother you that I know?"

"That my mom got knocked up after a one-night stand? That my dad turned out to be a criminal *and* an abusive prick? That my mom had to turn into a snitch to get us out of there?" She shrugged. "Nah, that's the fairy tale life every girl dreams about."

"I think it did your mom some good to tell me."

"Well, at least you got your first kiss."

"What are you talking about?"

"I told you, I heard everything. And right after you promised to be our knight in shining armor, things got real quiet. I figure that's when you guys did the lip-lock thing."

"You're a smart kid, but you got that part wrong."

"Whatever." Her face grew serious. "So how much danger are we really in?"

"Guess you really did hear everything."

"It's an old house, lots of cracks, and like I said, sound travels."

"I won't lie to you, Lizzy. You are in danger." His voice hardened. "But not for long." He turned to leave.

"Hey, Luke?"

He paused. "Yeah?"

"Be careful." She hesitated, and it quickly became clear that what she wanted to say next didn't come naturally. "I'll...I'll say a prayer for you."

"Say a prayer for them," Stone replied. "They're gonna need it."

TWENTY-FIVE

BACK OUT IN THE NIGHT, the Blazer's headlights punching holes in the darkness as they lit up the road and illuminated the swirling snowflakes that were a prelude to tomorrow's blizzard, Stone's resolve remained unbroken.

But he still had to wrestle with his demons.

He intended to kill again. That was the cold, hard truth. With Holly and Lizzy's lives threatened, he needed to put down the Bible, pick up a gun, and blow holes in some bastards who clearly had it coming.

Just one problem.

Thou shalt not kill.

Yeah, there it was. The Sixth Commandment. Kind of hard for a preacher to ignore.

His kills last night had been in self-defense. Scripture clearly indicated that resorting to lethal force to protect yourself was permitted. He felt no guilt about that. Come at him with guns blazing, expect to catch some return fire in the teeth. God didn't expect anyone to lay down and get slaughtered without a fight.

Most preachers believed the sixth commandment was

properly interpreted, *Thou shall not murder*. In other words, many millennia ago, God slapped a ban on planned, premeditated killing.

But that still posed a problem for Stone. Because right now, he planned on stopping at his house, loading up with some serious firepower, and heading into the swamp to terminate the threat against Holly and Lizzy. And that meant putting bullets into bodies.

If Carl and his creeps had only put their crosshairs on him, he wouldn't have been planning a kill 'em all rampage. He would have been content to weather the feud, praying that it died down and eventually just went away, only resorting to violence to protect himself if necessary.

But when their cyclone of hate sucked in those he cared about, it was time to go on the offensive. He could not just stand by and hope everything turned out okay. He had to make sure they were safe.

He just hoped the Good Lord understood that.

The road unfolded before him in a dark, gray ribbon with scattered bursts of white. A perfect metaphor for his soul. Darkness lurked within him, always ready to shred its way back to the surface like a wild beast breaking free from its cage. He had tried to tame that darkness by turning to the light, to a life of faith.

But he had only partially succeeded. Because it was now clear that the light was not enough to keep his darkness at bay forever.

He cut down a backroad that would bring him to the outskirts of Whisper Falls so he could stop at the church and check on Max before gearing up for his strike against the survivalists. As he drove, he found himself silently praying.

Lord, I'm not claiming that what I'm about to do is right, but I know that it needs to be done. So I guess I'm asking for forgiveness ahead of time, even though I know it doesn't work that way. But when it comes to wicked men loose in the world, sometimes grace and turn-the-other-cheek only go so far. I'm not walking away from you...but I can't walk away from what I have to do.

It was an honest prayer, perhaps the most honest one he had ever prayed.

But by the time he turned into the church parking lot and exited the truck into the snow-swirled night, God hadn't bothered responding.

———

Inside the church, Max curled up on the couch beside him, the dog's scarred-up head resting on Stone's thigh. He gently scratched the Shottie's ears as he told him everything, up to and including his plan to hunt down the survivalists tonight. He even told Max all about the conflicts of faith his lethal plan generated, as well as his determination to go through with it anyway.

The dog was a good listener, even if he couldn't offer any advice. When Stone finished his confession, the Shottie lifted his head and opened his jaws wide in a yawn so big, it reminded Stone of a lion getting ready to roar.

For some reason, the sight made him think of Samson, the strongest man in the Bible, and how he killed a lion with his bare hands, "tearing it apart like a young goat," according to the scriptural account. The long-haired Nazarite later slew one thousand Philistines with the jawbone of an ass. Yet he was still considered one of the great heroes of the Bible despite boasting a four-digit kill-count.

Clearly, God sometimes called warriors to slay the wicked.

Just like Stone intended to do tonight.

Maybe that was the answer to his prayer.

Or maybe he was just twisting scripture to find a divine sanction for his vigilante methods.

He pushed the troubling thoughts aside. There would be time enough later to sort it all out and pray for his soul.

Right now, he needed to put bullets into some bastards.

TWENTY-SIX

STONE SAID GOODBYE TO MAX, telling the dog he'd be back by morning, and that if he didn't make it, Holly would take care of him. The Shottie gave him a look that said, *I'll be here, man, getting hair all over the couch.*

He drove to his house and ducked under the yellow crime scene tape that seemed to have sprouted up everywhere like invasive weeds. Hard to believe it had been less than twenty-four hours since Carl's cronies had tried to bushwhack him in his own home. The thought pissed him off all over again. That, combined with them threatening of Holly and Lizzy, stoked his rage into white-hot coals.

He made his way down to the vault in the basement, broken glass and debris crunching under his boots. He was dressed in black to help him blend into the night with a layer of thermal underclothes tight against his skin to ward off the cold. There was a Kevlar combat vest cinched across his upper torso beneath his jacket.

He donned a shoulder rig designed to hold the Smith & Wesson Stealth Hunter .44 Magnum revolver. The

Smith & Wesson was a heavy piece to carry on a covert strike but he didn't care. He preferred six-guns and the Stealth Hunter was his favorite, so it was coming with him. He dropped speed-loaders into the deep, roomy cargo pockets of his insulated tactical pants.

Of course, the survivalists possessed full-auto weapons, and going up against submachine guns with nothing but a revolver was a fool's errand, and Stone was no fool. He knew he needed an autofire option.

He slung the Heckler & Koch UMP-45 across his back and slotted four 25-round magazines into various pockets on his person. He could have opted for the HK416 in 5.56X45mm NATO, but preferred the shorter length of the UMP for maneuverability. Making his way through the swamp and then most likely engaging in close quarters combat, those extra inches could make a difference. The HK416 was a great carbine but the UMP-45 was better suited for tonight's mission. He threaded a suppressor onto the barrel to give himself a quiet-kill option.

Next, he clipped a Benchmade Bedlam 860 folding tactical knife into his right hip pocket. The fully ambidextrous knife featured one-handed opening capability and the curved blade provided excellent defense in a knife fight. A little larger than your typical folding blade, which was one of the reasons Stone liked it so much. A bit oversized for everyday carry but perfect for a tactical operation.

He clipped a couple of fragmentation grenades to the combat webbing of his vest. If any of the swamp rats decided to hole up somewhere, tossing in a fragger was a good way to burn them out.

He closed the vault and double checked his inventory. He had 18 hollow-point cartridges for the .44 Magnum, 100 rounds of .45 for the HK UMP, plus the knife and grenades. If he couldn't take out a dozen survivalists with that, he should hang up his guns.

You already did that once.

He ignored the voice and walked back out into the night, ready for war.

TWENTY-SEVEN

BY THE TIME Stone pulled the Chevy Blazer off to the side of one of the roads that cut through the vast Sinkhole Hollow Swamp region, his blood had cooled enough to make him realize he couldn't just go charging the survivalist compound like a one-man wrecking machine, blowing away anything and anyone that moved.

God might forgive him for gunning down the guilty. But God would be pretty damned displeased if he killed any innocents. Carl and Blackbeard had explicitly threatened Holly and Lizzy and Stone remained committed to putting them down. But despite the survivalists' reputation as a bunch of trigger-happy cutthroats who did Mason Xavier's dirty work in exchange for blood money, Stone had no concrete proof that everyone currently residing on the compound deserved a bullet.

So instead of a hard-charging, rock 'n' roll assault, he decided to switch gears and go with a soft probe. Depending on what he found would determine if just a couple of men died tonight...or all of them.

So yeah, start soft and go hard later. That was the plan.

It was a little after midnight, the sickle-moon shrouded behind the thick cloud cover that continued to leak swirling snowflakes as a precursor to tomorrow's blizzard. No wind yet, but the air was still very cold, dipping down toward zero. Stone's breath plumed into the darkness like an exhalation of smoke.

He shifted his gear until it hung from his tall frame as comfortably as possible, then moved into the swamp. The crackling crunch of snow and ice under his boots sounded like a bull moose stomping in the cold silence of the night. Nothing to worry about yet though; he was still two miles from the compound. When he got closer, he would focus on being quieter.

He navigated the terrain at a steady pace. The swamp would have been nearly impenetrable in the non-winter months, but the brackish water was frozen solid, making travel relatively easy. He skirted the jagged stumps poking up through the surface like rotted teeth, dodged the deadfalls that seemed to be piled up everywhere, and bulled through thickets when necessary. He could feel sweat soaking his scalp beneath the black skullcap he wore—no cowboy hat for this mission—but didn't dare take it off. At these low temperatures, the sweat would freeze almost instantly and turn the top of his head into an icicle.

With the moon and stars camouflaged behind the clouds, the swamp was a dark place. But Stone had been trained to operate in the dark. His night vision worked just fine, allowing him to decipher all the blurry shapes and looming shadows surrounding him. The swamp was unfriendly but it failed to incite any fear in him. He had survived frozen tundra and thick jungles in his past and Sinkhole Hollow Swamp was just a twisted, tangled combination of the two.

Keeping a steady but not-rushing pace, he reached the perimeter of the compound in just under ninety minutes. He first saw the lights through the trees, then as he cautiously edged closer, he spotted the chain-link fence that encircled the camp. The dual-coiled razor-wire on top gave the compound a prison aesthetic.

Stone had reconnoitered the compound through satellite photos. Not the blurry, low-grade images available on the internet either. He still had plenty of contacts from his warrior days—men who liked him, men who respected him, men who owed him. A quick call to an intelligence agency buddy and a short time later, crisp, high-resolution photos from one of the hundreds of surveillance satellites floating through space had showed up on his phone. Thank God for modern technology and thank God for friends in the right places.

The compound consisted of 80 acres of land that had formed a natural, almost perfectly square clearing in the swamp. The dirt road snaked around to approach the main gate from the north. Inside, a dozen small cabins squatted in the northeast corner while the northwest corner consisted of a firing range with a large dirt berm for a backstop. Behind the berm was a Conex shipping container and a small building that sprouted with various antennas and satellite dishes.

To the east lay the motor pool area, while the entire southern end of the property seemed devoted to a dirt track, presumably so the survivalists could practice vehicular tactics and defensive driving. Various sheds and Quonset huts were sprinkled across the grounds in no discernable pattern or purpose. Probably safe to assume that at least one of the buildings housed the armory and explosives.

Stone took up concealed position behind the tentacle-like root system of a fallen tree on the eastern side of the camp. He didn't move for the next hour and in that time, saw only one sentry patrolling the perimeter, walking a beaten path just inside the wire fence with an M4 carbine cradled in his arms. The survivalist wore fingerless gloves despite the cold so that he could get on the trigger fast if need be. He kept raising his hands and blowing warm breath on his exposed fingertips to ward off frostbite.

If the man had not been the enemy, Stone might have actually felt sorry for him. Pulling guard duty in the middle of a cold, snowy, winter night sucked. But with Holly and Lizzy's lives on the line, he was fresh out of compassion and sympathy.

Satisfied that there was just the one roving patrol on duty tonight, Stone waited for the sentry to pass by, then waited another ten minutes for good measure before making his move.

The survivalists had cleared out the trees near the fence-line, creating a barren no-man's-land between the fence and the woods that was void of cover for fifty yards. A smart defensive decision, since it meant nobody could use a tree to scale the fence. And with the razor-wire forming a slashing crown, a simple climb-over wasn't in the cards either.

Since he couldn't go over, Stone decided to go under.

He crept through the woods until he reached an area with no security lights, just beyond the motor pool. It was as good a breach point as any.

He found a long branch, then crossed the exposed stretch of ground and crouched between two support posts, where the fence would be slackest. Working quickly, he used his knife to dig out a space beneath the bottom row of links, then wedged the branch under the fence, using it as a lever to force the lower part of the fence to rise, the links bending upward to form a gap in the shape of a rough half-circle. It gave him just enough room to claw his way underneath.

He was covered with cold dirt and starting to sweat beneath his layers of clothing, but he had successfully penetrated the compound.

He climbed to his feet and brushed off the frozen clumps of soil clinging to him. Then he readjusted his gear from where it had shifted during his low-crawl under the fence and moved off through the darkness, looking for the roaming sentry.

He had no plans to kill the guard at this point in time —that might change later, depending on what he found out—but he needed to neutralize him so that his hole under the fence wasn't discovered and an alarm raised.

Skilled at hunting men, it didn't take long for Stone to locate the guy. He was patrolling the southern perimeter, walking on the dirt track. There were no lights back here —at least none that were on right now—but the sentry made the mistake of firing up a cigarette and the glowing cancer-stick gave away his position.

Stone zeroed in on that red flare like a heat-seeking missile coming in hot on target.

He drew the Smith & Wesson .44 Magnum, planning to club the man into unconsciousness with the heavy barrel. The sentry's footsteps crunching on the frozen turf masked the sound of Stone's approach. As the guy took another long drag on his cigarette, Stone crept close enough to be the man's shadow. He raised the revolver like a bludgeon, ready to slam it against the back of the guy's skull.

At the last moment, the sentry sensed the movement behind him. He spun around, cigarette flying from his mouth, and tried to muscle the M4 into play.

Too late.

The blow meant for the back of his skull instead smashed into his mouth. The matte-black steel of the Magnum's barrel pulped his lips and splintered his teeth with a meaty crunch. The sentry went down hard. Blood drooled out onto the ground, melting the snow with liquid heat. A few feet away, the cigarette winked out, much like the light in the man's eyes. The guy would be out cold for quite some time and when he woke up, he would need an orthodontist and a concussion specialist.

Stone used the sentry's belt and bootlaces to tie him to one of the fence posts. He didn't bother gagging him; no screams were going to come out of that mangled horror show of a mouth. Besides, this was the backside of the compound; even if the guy managed to scream, nobody would hear him.

With the sentry out of commission and all trussed up, Stone worked his way back toward the front of the compound. He planned to avoid the cabins until he had dug around and gathered information. At the very least, Carl and Blackbeard were going to die tonight. For Holly and Lizzy's sake, he was putting them down and nothing short of divine intervention would save them. And Stone strongly suspected God had better things to do tonight than waste time saving their sorry asses.

Whether or not the rest of them died depended entirely on what he found.

He hiked down the western side of the compound, heading toward the firing range. When he reached the Conex container, he would cut over to the electrical building and start his search there. It seemed like a logical place for a computer station and he possessed enough hacking skills to infiltrate their electronic files. With luck, he would find records indicating just how guilty or innocent these ragtag survivalists actually were.

But when he reached the Conex box, he saw something that stopped him dead in his tracks and the chill that went through him had nothing to do with the winter weather.

TWENTY-EIGHT

STONE STARED down at the pink teddy bear lying crumpled on the frozen ground in front of the shipping container. One black-button eye was missing and stuffing seeped from the torn cavity. A muddy boot-print was stomped across the bear's plush belly, grinding it down into the cold dirt.

What was a child's toy doing on a survivalist compound that by all accounts did not allow women or children?

Stone examined the door of the Conex box. There were a dozen holes drilled through the metal, each hole approximately a half-inch in diameter, spaced evenly apart in three rows, forming a neat rectangular pattern about five feet up. Unless he was sorely mistaken—and he seriously hoped that he was—Stone knew what they were for.

Ventilation holes.

He cursed under his breath.

The door featured a padlock but it was unsecured, the clasp hanging open. He pulled it off and dropped it on the ground. He then worked the levers on the right-hand door, moving slowly to minimize any metallic creaks from rusty hinges that might give away his presence, and cracked it open enough to slip inside.

Once he was in, he pulled the door shut behind him, activated his flashlight, and shined it around the interior. It was a risk—the light could seep out the ventilation holes and give him away—but he needed to check things out.

The box was your standard size shipping container, eight feet wide, eight and a half feet high, and twenty feet long. There wasn't much inside, but there was enough to make the vein in Stone's jaw start throbbing. He clenched his teeth and shook his head as righteous rage flooded through him.

There was a dirty, stained mattress on the floor covered with a pile of Army surplus blankets. A small space heater squatted in one corner, a portable camping toilet occupied the other corner. Scattered across the floor were a couple of dog-eared children's books, a purple hairbrush, and another stuffed animal—this one a white unicorn with a rainbow emblazoned on his chest. Various articles of little girls' clothing were strewn about, much of it ripped and torn. More ventilation holes were bored through the back wall.

Stone felt sickened and found it hard to breathe.

This wasn't a shipping container.

It was a fucking cage for little kids.

Stone saw scratches that looked like the desperate clawing of tiny fingernails. It reminded him of the photos he had seen of the ovens at Auschwitz. Terrified people hopelessly clawing for salvation. Even the air in here smelled like fear, darkness, and despair. An evil stench that permeated everything.

Stone turned off his flashlight as he stumbled out of the Conex box and sucked in a deep lungful of fresh air, seeking to cleanse himself from the unholy smell. He had experienced the scent before, many times. In Afghanistan, Russia, and other hellish hotspots all across the globe where humans preyed on their own kind. It was a stench he had hoped to never smell again.

But here it was, poisoning the mountain air in a back-woods swamp of northern New York.

Stone's head whipped to the right as the door to the electrical building suddenly opened. He retreated into the darkness behind the shipping container as a man appeared in the doorway, little more than a silhouette against the backlight from the building.

"Hank!" the man called, raising his voice louder than a normal conversational tone but lower than a full shout. Probably didn't want to wake up his buddies racked out on their bunks in the cabins, which weren't that far away. "Hank, you out there?"

Stone filled his hands with the H&K UMP-45. He kept his finger off the bang-switch for now, but thumbed off the safety. A round nestled in the chamber, ready to dispense lethal justice if Stone judged it necessary.

"All right, Hank," the guy in the shack said. "If you can hear me, coffee's on. Come get yourself a cup and put some heat on your bones." He chuckled as if that was the funniest thing he had ever said and hell, maybe it was. He then added, "You can scope out the footage from our hunt the other night. Got some great shots of that little lamb going down hard."

He stepped back into the building and closed the door.

Stone counted off three minutes before making his move. He figured Hank was the roving sentry currently strapped to a fence post out back, but he wanted to make sure nobody else showed up before he crashed the party and started looking for answers.

He approached the electronics shack cautiously, the HK submachine gun tucked tight against his shoulder, muzzle aimed at the door in case the occupant reappeared. If that happened, a couple of suppressed shots would push him back inside, and Stone wouldn't bat an eye at the kill. The Conex box and the implications of its contents, combined with chilling phrases like "our hunt" and "little lamb going down hard," strongly hinted that something vile had taken place and there were no innocents in this compound.

But he reached the door without needing to fire any shots—he expected that would change before this night ended—and checked the knob. It turned easily. The guy inside hadn't bothered locking the door behind him.

That simplified things. Stone had expected to use a .45 caliber knock to gain access, but now he could just walk right in and introduce himself.

He opened the door like he owned the place and stepped inside.

The heat was a welcome relief from the cold and snow outside. A half-wall bisected the building. The front half where Stone was standing looked like a videographer's storage room, stuffed with cameras, tripods, lenses, and such. Pine-plank wall shelving held user manuals, how-to books, and an assortment of DVDs. One shelf even contained a stack of VHS tapes that probably qualified for antique status.

In the other half of the room, three computer monitors —one large one, two slightly smaller—occupied the far wall. A long bench spanned from one side of the room to the other, covered with keyboards, hard drives, mouse pads, USB drives, DVD-R burners, and a rat's nest of tangled, twisted, multicolored wires running in every direction.

And up on the main monitor, the image frozen in

crystal-clear, hi-definition clarity, was Sadie Wadford.

A man wearing a wolf mask had a fist in her hair, yanking her head back. His other hand prepared to drag a knife across the taut flesh of her exposed throat.

The survivalist who had opened the door a few minutes ago and called to Hank, the sentry, sat on a rolling chair with his back to Stone. His fingers pecked away at a keyboard in front of him. Up on the monitor, Stone saw some color correction applied to the image, a subtle lightening of the shadows that made Sadie's terrified face stand out even more.

The computer guy didn't even turn around when Stone walked in. Just called out, "Hey, Hank, where were you? Hollered for you a couple minutes ago. Cold as a dead Eskimo out there, huh?" He waved to his left where a coffee pot sat on an electric burner. "Help yourself to some java and pull up a chair. I'll give you a sneak peek of the footage I put together tonight. As you can see..." He gestured toward the main monitor. "...I'm just getting to the good stuff." He chuckled, low and nasty. "Well, the good stuff that happened after the *other* good stuff."

As Stone stepped through the opening in the half-wall, he noticed the Browning Hi-Power 9mm pistol lying on the bench next to a cup of steaming coffee, well within arm's reach for the survivalist.

"I'm not Hank," Stone said as he pressed the tip of the HK's suppressor against the back of the man's neck. "And I don't want any coffee."

The guy froze, all tense and stiff from the cold circle of steel nudged against his nape. "Who are you?"

"You can call me Preacher."

"Shit," the man mumbled. "You're that guy."

"Yeah, I'm that guy."

"Carl *really* wants you dead."

"The feeling's mutual. But I'll deal with your boss

later. Right now, I want you to tell me about the Conex box outside and what Sadie Wadford is doing on your computer screen." Stone prodded him with the UMP-45, making him rock forward a few inches. "So start talking."

"Sorry, preacher, but I can't do that. Carl will kill me if he finds out I talked."

"The only thing Carl is going to find out is just how hot Hell is," Stone replied. He gave the survivalist another shove with the HK. "I'm the one with a gun to your head. Worry about me."

"You don't know Carl."

Lowering his voice to a dangerous growl, Stone said, "And you don't know me. I've done things that would give the devil nightmares. Start talking or start losing body parts."

Without warning, the man went for his gun. A fool's play, one of the stupidest Stone had ever seen. What was the guy thinking? Stone had him point-blank, dead to rights. The dumb bastard didn't have a snowball's chance in hell of succeeding.

That didn't stop him from trying though.

He threw his head to the side, trying to get it out of the line of fire. At the same time, his hand shot across the bench, knocking over the coffee cup. Brown liquid spilled everywhere as his fingers scrabbled for the butt of the Browning Hi-Power.

With one quick motion, Stone shifted the HK's aim and pumped a single round through the top of the man's hand. The bullet exited his palm, blowing it in open like a .45 caliber crucifixion.

The man jerked his hand back. Thanks to the suppressor, the shot had been quiet, but the survivalist looked like he was about to let out an agonized howl.

Stone slammed the barrel against the back of the man's head again. "You scream, you die. So unless you want your face splattered all over that monitor, you'd better bite your tongue real damn hard."

The guy gulped hard and managed to swallow the pain; nothing escaped his lips but a few mewling whimpers.

"Now start talking. My patience is wearing thin and when my patience gets thin, my trigger finger starts getting twitchy."

The guy stopped stalling. His name was Jeb and he spilled his guts about the whole operation. As he talked, Stone felt himself growing sick and angry. White-hot embers of rage burned deep down inside and the more Jeb talked, the more a cold wind fanned those embers into savage flames that threatened to consume his soul.

They called the "game" Wolves and Lambs. They abducted young girls—the lambs—and raped them, then turned them loose in the swamp to be hunted down and slaughtered by the survivalists, who all wore wolf masks to protect their identities. Jeb's job was to capture the whole thing on film, then edit it all together to create a sickeningly graphic but well-produced child porn/snuff video that they then sold on the dark web.

Stone had smashed numerous human-trafficking and sex-slave rings back in his warrior days, but never anything as sick as this. These bastards had taken evil to a whole new level and committed the kind of vile sins that even God would struggle to forgive.

Unfortunately for them, Stone wasn't God and he had no intention of forgiving anything.

"Who came up with the idea for this sick shit?" he asked.

"It was Carl's boy, Dez. He...he likes 'em young."

Stone's jaw clenched. This compound was a cesspool of evil. It needed to be burned to the ground until there was nothing left but ashes.

Jeb continued, "The first time, we took one of the girls from the reservation. After Dez...you know..."

"I think the word you're looking for is 'rape'," Stone said coldly.

Jeb sighed. "Yeah, that. After Dez finished with the girl, we weren't quite sure what to do with her, you know? Wasn't like any of us had done that sort of thing before. But then Dez had this idea that we should let her go in the swamp, give her a head-start, and then hunt her down. Carl thought that was great. Said it would be good training."

"How'd it turn into a business?"

"That first time, Dez filmed the whole thing on his cell phone. He uploaded the video to one of those sites on the dark web that specializes in violent, nasty stuff and it was a huge hit. Dez realized we could make some serious cash with these kinds of videos. Carl was all for it, one thing led to another, and bam, Wolves and Lambs Production was born."

"How many girls have you done this to?"

Jeb shrugged. "I dunno. Not that many."

"Unless you want to know what a bullet in the back of the head feels like, I'm gonna need you to be more specific."

"Maybe six?" Jeb nodded. "Yeah, that sounds about right. We've only been doing it for a couple of years and we usually do a hunt every four months or so."

"It's not a hunt," Stone rasped through clenched teeth. "It's the rape and murder of little girls."

Jeb shrugged again. "Semantics."

"And you just edit the footage?"

"I do it all," Jeb replied. "I shoot the video, edit, produce it, pick the music...everything." He sounded proud of himself.

"So you just work behind the scenes, or do you participate in the hunt?"

Jeb hesitated for a couple seconds, then decided the truth was the best way to go. "We all participate," he said. "Carl requires it."

Stone had heard enough. "Thanks for the information."

"Please, man, don't kil—"

He never finished the request, because Stone shot him in the back of the head.

The corpse flopped forward in a splattering of blood, then slowly slid out of the chair as gravity combined with dead weight and pulled the body down to the floor like a string-cut puppet.

Stone sat down in the freshly-vacated chair, letting the HK hang from its sling as he worked the controls to activate the video. Up on the central monitor, Sadie Wadford was about to be killed and Stone hoped this unedited footage would show her murderer unmasked.

He steeled himself for what he was about to see, gritted his teeth, and un-paused the video.

He suffered through Sadie's horrible death, feeling a holy hatred welling up inside him as he watched her killer raise his wolf-masked face to the moon and let loose a bellowing howl of bloodlust.

Then, as the film continued to roll and the savage cry echoed through the silvered darkness of the swamp, the killer lowered his head. As he stared down at Sadie's butchered body bleeding out at his feet, he lifted a hand and removed the mask from his face.

Stone recoiled as if he'd been struck in the face with a sledgehammer. As he stared at the man behind the mask, the man who had murdered Sadie Wadford, he realized that after tonight, Whisper Falls would never be the same.

TWENTY-NINE

STONE SPENT the next thirty minutes rummaging through the computer files. It was all there. Every little girl, every violation, every hunt, every kill. Both the finished product and the raw footage. Client lists and banking account numbers. He even found the doctored, deep-faked videos they had planted on Walter Nugent's computer to frame the coroner for Sadie's rape and murder.

He forwarded it all to one of his old contacts in the FBI. The head of this unholy hydra might be right here on this compound, but the tentacles slithered further than Stone could handle on his own. He would burn out the sickness poisoning his own backyard, but the FBI was better equipped to smoke out the far-flung threads.

Satisfied that he had put into motion the actions necessary to take down this nest of vipers, Stone rose to his feet, wishing he had some gasoline to pour all over the video equipment and set it ablaze. Every foul thing he had viewed the last half-hour deserved to be burned to ashes. The images he had witnessed would haunt him forever. He would hear the screams of dying children in his nightmares for the rest of his life. Their tortured faces would take up residence in his soul, right next to his dead daughter.

Allowing his thoughts to turn inward dampened his reflexes. So when the door to the shack crashed open and Hank charged in with his M4 raised and ready to fire, Stone was a half-second too slow to get the UMP-45 into play.

Hank's face was a broken, blood-and-pulp horror show from Stone's pistol-whipping. Hate burned hot in his eyes. Stone didn't know how the sentry had freed himself—there were many ways to slip bonds and the survivalists were probably trained in most of them—but that didn't matter right now.

All that mattered was that Hank was here and the full-auto burst he triggered was loud enough to wake the dead. Every man on this compound would converge on the shack in ninety seconds, maybe less.

Quiet time was over.

Stone dropped to his knees while simultaneously throwing himself to the side. The salvo of 5.56mm rounds sizzling his way missed him save for one bullet that caught him in the upper left arm. It tore through his jacket and gouged a bloody trench in his flesh. The rest of the slugs slammed into the monitors, smashing them to pieces.

Stone ignored the burning pain and cut loose with the HK. The rising burst lashed Hank in the thigh before carving diagonally across his pelvis, abdomen, and chest. The powerful punch of the .45 caliber projectiles hurled him back out the door and into the cold night, dead by the time he hit the frozen dirt.

Stone scrambled to his feet and hustled outside, stepping over Hank's body as shouts of alarm sounded from the direction of the cabins. He hustled back over to the

Conex container and took up position behind it just as security lights powered on, flooding the compound with harsh, bright illumination.

Stone cursed the lights. The odds were currently 10-to-1 against him. He could have used the cover of darkness to give himself an edge. The lights were arrayed at various positions all across the compound, so shooting them all out wasn't an option. He briefly considered taking out the one closest to him but didn't want to risk giving away his position. Right now his only advantage —besides superior combat skills—was that they didn't know exactly where he was.

He performed a tactical magazine exchange to maximize the number of rounds in the HK, then quickly checked his wound. It was deep, the meat ripped open, but it had missed the bone. It stung like hell, but he could ignore it for now and stitch it up later. Another scar for his collection.

Assuming he survived.

He risked a glance around the corner of the Conex container, keeping his head low. Four men came from the direction of the cabins, dashing through the pools of light. Summoned by the sound of gunfire, they ran toward the computer shack. They stayed in a tightly-clustered formation, a tactical error. Spreading out would have made it harder to pick them off.

They ran up to the dead sentry and formed a circle around their fallen comrade. "It's Hank!" one of them exclaimed, as if the others couldn't see that for themselves.

"Holy crap!" one of the others said. "Somebody shot the shit outta him."

Yeah, Stone thought. *And now it's time to shoot some more shit.*

He leaned out around the edge of the Conex box and

unleashed a full-auto firestorm downrange, sweeping the muzzle back and forth in a tightly-controlled figure-8 pattern.

The bunched-up survivalists paid for their mistake with their lives. Hot lead buzz-sawed through them like meat cleavers through raw meat. They shuddered and jerked their way through spastic death-dances that sent them corkscrewing to the ground with blood spurting from all the bullet holes.

He caught movement on his left peripheral as his submachine gun ran dry. His had swiveled as he ejected the spent magazine and spotted three men, fanned out in a single-file line, crossing from the cover of a Quonset hut to the rear of the computer shack. They fired from the hip as they ran, bullets kicking up snowy tufts of clod in front of him. More rounds hammered the shipping container. It sounded like hard rain smacking against a metal roof.

Clearly they had identified his position. The hip-firing was designed to keep his head down until they could reach the cover of the shack, at which point they would no doubt launch some sort of counterstrike to neutralize him.

He slapped home a fresh magazine and swung the HK toward the trio. He ignored the incoming rounds. They were hasty, undisciplined. If they managed to hit him, it would be through sheer luck.

He triggered a short burst. The middle man threw up his arms and went spinning to the side. He crashed to the ground, limbs splayed out like he was trying to make a snow angel before he died.

The front guy reached the cover of the shack, but the rear gunman still had several yards to go.

He didn't make it.

Stone hit him with a high burst, bullets punching through the gunner's neck and head. The high-powered impacts kicked him sideways as if he'd been struck by the fist of God.

A bellow of rage thundered from behind the shack. "Damn you, preacher!"

Stone wasn't sure how they knew it was him. Maybe they were just making an assumption. After all, he had shot Blackbeard in the leg yesterday and sent him limping back to the compound with a stern warning.

More movement to the right. Two men at the far edge of the lights, running hell-bent-for-leather toward the motor pool. From this distance, Stone couldn't be sure, but they looked like Carl and Dez.

Real tough guys, Stone thought. Father and son make a run for it while the cannon-fodder minions hold off the enemy.

Just another sin to add to their running tally.

He vowed not to let them get away.

Behind the shack, the survivalist continued to snarl his fury. "I'm gonna kill you, preacher! Gonna fill your ass with so much hot shit that God himself won't recognize you when you get to the pearly gates."

The hell with this.

Stone needed to move fast if he wanted to nail Carl and Dez. Screw around with this asshole too long and the father-son duo would flee the compound in the first vehicle they got their hands on. And once they got away, there was a damn good chance they would pay Holly and Lizzy a visit.

Stone could not allow that to happen.

So he charged.

He knew it was the last thing the survivalist expected him to do. And sometimes the unexpected could produce an opening. A chance to turn the tables and end the game.

Stone didn't cut loose with a kamikaze yell or anything like that. He just started running.

His boots dug into the frozen ground, propelling him forward like a human missile. He kept the UMP-45 tight to his shoulder as he swiftly crossed the gap between the Conex box and the computer shack.

"You messed with the wrong swamp boys, preacher! You're a dumbass sheep playing with the goddamned wolves!"

Stone almost grinned to himself. The man's bellicose bellowing covered the sound of Stone's approaching footsteps. Death was rushing for him at a fast sprint and the survivalist didn't even know it because he couldn't keep his mouth shut.

A tactical error. One from which he would never recover.

Time to die, asshole, Stone thought as he neared the corner of the shack.

"Hey, preacher! How 'bout we put down our guns and settle this man to—"

Stone rounded the corner and shoved the HK's muzzle into the man's face. "I don't think so."

The survivalist's eyes bulged wide in surprise. Then his eyes disappeared—along with most of his skull—as Stone pulled the trigger and put a half-dozen .45 slugs into his head at pointblank range.

The body hadn't even hit the ground before Stone took off running again. As he headed toward the motor pool, he heard the throaty rumble of an engine cranking to life. He forced his feet to move even faster, praying he didn't slip on an icy patch and go down in a bone-breaking sprawl.

He came around a Quonset hut in time to see an olive-drab Chevy pickup truck with oversized tires, a brush guard, fake smokestacks, and an auxiliary fuel tank come ripping down the gravel road that snaked along the perimeter of the compound.

The pickup was almost upon him, motor roaring like an angry beast. Dez was behind the wheel while Carl rode shotgun.

Spotting Stone, Dez jerked the truck to the left, trying to clip him. Stone jumped back, the vehicle narrowly missing the corner of the building.

As the truck rumbled past, Stone snapped the HK into play, stitching a rising burst that tattooed holes in the tail-gate, tore into the auxiliary tank, and blew apart the back window. He saw the silhouetted figures of the father-son duo duck their heads and hunch their shoulders as the glass exploded around them, but they gave no indication of being hit.

The truck accelerated, making a break for the front gate as gasoline spewed from the punctured auxiliary tank and flooded the cargo bed.

Stone fired another burst at the fleeing Chevy, aiming low to take out the tires. He kept the trigger slammed back, emptying the magazine. The bullets chewed apart the rubber until nothing but black shreds hung from the metal rims. The wheels plowed into the gravel and the truck sloughed back and forth a couple of times as Dez fought for control.

Before the Chevy lurched to a stop, Stone had a grenade in his fist. He pulled the pin and fast-pitched it into the back of the truck.

Carl opened his door and scrambled out of the cab a second before the grenade detonated. The concussive explosion lifted him off his feet and tossed him onto the shoulder of the road. He landed hard and rolled to a jarring stop against a snow-frosted tree stump. He rebounded and clutched at his side, grimacing. Looked like maybe he'd broken a rib.

Stone heard him shout something—it sounded like "Dez!"—but it was hard to hear over the blast.

The son was not as lucky as the father.

The explosion ignited the leaking fuel and sent tendrils of flaming gas splashing through the shattered back window. By the time Dez got his door open and stumbled away from the burning truck, his head was haloed in fire, and he screamed like a dying rabbit.

Stone felt nothing as he watched the survivalist burn. He deserved it for what he done to those little girls. Sometimes justice is red-hot and raw.

Dez slapped at his engulfed head, but the gasoline continued to burn, blackening his flesh. His eyeballs boiled in their sockets.

Stone walked toward the dying man as the truck continued to blaze like a bonfire in the night. He let the empty submachine gun dangle from its sling as he drew the Smith & Wesson six-gun. The flames caused orange sparks to dance off the black metal.

As he approached the fire-engulfed Dez, he saw Carl rise to one knee and claw frantically for a pistol holstered on his side.

Long before that pistol even started to clear leather, the .44 bucked in Stone's fist and sent Magnum thunder rolling through the night.

Carl threw his arms out and thudded backwards as if he'd been kicked in the chest by a wild stallion. The hollow-point drilled him in the center of his torso, just below the sternum, and dumped him in a sitting position against the stump. Almost immediately, the snow beneath him began to melt from all the blood running out of the gaping exit wound in his back.

He wasn't quite dead yet, but he would be very soon.

With the father out of commission, Stone turned his attention back to the son. Carl might have been the leader of this mongrel pack of psychos, but Dez was the one with pedophilic urges, the first one to rape and kill, the one who came up with the idea to hunt the "lambs."

If not for the evil sickness lurking in the darkness of Dez's soul, Sadie Wadford—along with all those other girls—would still be alive.

Now the son of a bitch was wrapped in a living hell, paying for his sins.

The fire had spread to his clothes. Cocooned in flames, his screams silenced by scorched vocal cords and blistered lips, he toppled over like a burning witch cut loose from the stake and writhed across the ground in agony.

Stone dug deep and managed to find a tiny shred of mercy. He raised the revolver and put a single shot between Dez's smoking eye sockets, ending his misery. It was one bullet more than the bastard deserved, as far as Stone was concerned, but somehow it still felt like the right thing to do. The body twitched a few times and then became still, the evil snuffed out, the corpse now content to cook.

Stone lowered the Smith & Wesson as he walked back over to Carl, slouched painfully against the tree stump, both hands clutched together over the hole in his center. Blood seeped between the clasped fingers in little red rivulets.

Even with death just moments away, the leader of the survivalists glared up at Stone with angry eyes. No remorse, no regret, no shame. Just rage and hate. A man who had done wicked things and remained proud of them.

Stone cocked the hammer on the .44. No point in dragging this out. "Any last words?"

Carl tried to hawk a bloody globule of spit at Stone's boots but only managed to spit on his own pants. "You might've beat us," he said, the words tight and clipped with pain through red-flecked teeth. "But winning a war comes at a cost."

"You really should save your breath," Stone said. "You're gonna need it to beg God for forgiveness."

"Yeah, that's right," Carl replied. "In all the killin' you been doing, I lost track that you're supposed to be some kind of holy man."

"That's right." Stone brought the gun up. "You fucked with the wrong preacher."

"See ya in Hell," Carl snarled. "Right along with those two bitches."

Stone hesitated for a fraction of a second, wanting to ask him what he meant by that. But deep down, he already knew.

...winning a war comes at a cost.

Fear like he hadn't felt since his daughter died reached up and strangled his throat with a cold, choking fist.

He pulled the trigger. The hammer snapped forward and sent a hollow-point sizzling through Carl's skull. The snow on top of the stump vanished beneath a hot spray of blood and brains.

Stone replaced the spent cartridges in the .44's cylinder before sliding it back into its holster and then charged the HK with a fresh magazine. Weapons topped off, he quickly scoured the compound and checked all the fallen survivalists.

The headcount confirmed his fear.

Blackbeard was missing.

Heart in his throat, he raced back to his truck.

THIRTY

THE CHEVY BLAZER rammed through the night at speeds far too dangerous for the weather conditions. At least two inches of snow had fallen since midnight, greasing the roads. The plows and salt trucks clearly had not worked their magic on Route 30 yet. The road was little more than two narrow strips of blacktop covered with accumulating snowfall.

Stone didn't care. He put the Chevy into four-wheel-drive and pushed the truck as fast as he dared, trusting the tires to stick to the pavement and fighting to control the fishtailing when they didn't.

He risked taking one hand off the steering wheel just long enough to press the button on his cell phone to call Holly again.

No answer. Just like the other thirteen times he tried to call.

God, don't do this to me. Don't you dare take them away from me, too.

He didn't make any hollow, desperate promises. No vows to swear less or drink less or give more money to the church. The Lord didn't work that way. Stone just said his prayer and left it at that. God would either listen or He wouldn't.

He tried Lizzy's cell as he passed the sign for the airport. It rang and rang like some kind of taunt, warning him that something was terribly wrong at the Bennett house, then went to voicemail.

"Damn it!" Stone wanted to smash his phone against the windshield in frustration. Instead, he tossed it on the passenger seat, grabbed the wheel with both hands, and drove even faster.

The headlights stabbed holes in the pre-dawn darkness as he reached Holly's house. He took the turn into the driveway too fast, the Chevy sliding sideways and ending up in the middle of their front lawn with ruts torn in the frozen turf. The truck shifted heavily to the left for a moment, threatening to roll, but then settled back down on its tires.

Stone exited the cab with the Smith & Wesson .44 in his hand. He saw boot-prints—far too large to be Holly's or Lizzy's—on the walkway and steps leading to the front door. There were no lights on, but candle-flame flickered behind the drawn curtains in the living room.

"Holly!" he shouted, crossing the lawn with the revolver at a ready position. "Liz!"

"Luke!" Holly called out. "We're in here!"

Relief flooded through him. They were alive, even if he could hear the strain in her voice.

As he raced up the steps, he saw the front door hanging crooked in its frame, hinges partly torn from the jamb where someone had forced it open. Stone vowed that if Blackbeard had hurt them in any way, he would tear the survivalist into so many pieces they would need a garbage bag instead of a coffin for his funeral.

He burst through the door with the .44 Magnum sweeping for a target.

A moment later he lowered the gun.

Blackbeard was sprawled on the floor in front of the couch. Two bullet holes dotted his chest. A third hole, jagged and splintered, gaped just above his right eye. The floor beneath him was soaked with blood.

Holly was curled up on the couch, arms wrapped around Lizzy, who was herself wrapped in a blanket, yet still shivering. The aftereffect of shock combined with an adrenalin dump. Two candles burned on the coffee table and Holly's Springfield XDS-9mm laid between them. Three spent shell casings littered the floor.

Stone holstered the Smith & Wesson, stepped over Blackbeard's body, and crouched down in front of the two people who mattered most to him. He gently put a hand on Holly's leg. Nothing sexual; just a comforting touch. "You okay?" he asked.

"We're okay." She gave him a quick smile. "You're a little late for the party."

"Sorry." He looked down at the blood spattered across the front of him. "I was busy having one of my own."

Holly looked at the blood, then looked back at his face, but didn't say anything.

"I tried calling you," he said.

"Phones are dead. Power went out shortly after you left, so we couldn't charge them."

Lizzy lifted her head. "Is it over?" she asked, her shivering causing her voice to tremble. "Are we safe now?"

Stone nodded. "You're safe, kiddo."

Holly locked eyes with him. "Are you sure?" she asked quietly. "You got them all?"

"There's just one left."

"What are you going to do about him?"

Stone rose to his feet. "I think it's time to call the sheriff."

THIRTY-ONE

STONE LEANED against a white birch tree at the top of Whisper Falls and waited for Sheriff Camden to show up. A few more inches of snow had fallen but he had managed to hike up the trail without too much difficulty and he had no doubt the sheriff would do the same. But after today, when the full force of the pre-Christmas blizzard slammed the region and buried the mountains under three feet of snow, nobody was getting up to the waterfall until spring.

Stone raised his head and squinted against the soft-but-steady flakes drifting down from the thick, leaden clouds blanketing the sky. It was an hour past dawn but the sun clearly had no intention of making an appearance today. The morning was cold and gray and would only worsen as the storm moved up the coast.

He knew Camden would come. The lawman really had no choice, given the phone call Stone had made.

"This is Sheriff Camden."

"Camden, it's Luke Stone. I have proof that Nugent didn't kill Sadie Wadford."

"What the hell are you babbling about, Stone?"

"Nugent didn't do it. He was set up."

"Then who did it?"

"I'm not talking about this over the phone."

"Where are you?"

"I hiked up to Whisper Falls. Needed to clear my head."

"Don't go anywhere. I'll come to you."

Stone gazed at all the pine branches drooping around him, the weight of the snow dragging them toward the ground. The snow muffled sounds up here, giving the place an almost tomblike feel. To his right, a snowshoe hare scampered across the fresh powder, kicking up little puffs with its large hind feet. Given the coy-wolves roaming these woods, Stone wondered if the rabbit would live to see tomorrow.

Thinking of the hare being hunted and killed made Stone think of the "wolves and lambs" hunts the survivalists had engaged in—and then profited from. It sickened him all over again. He wished Camden would hurry up so he could show him the evidence and get this over with.

Stone wasn't sure how the sheriff would react to the revelation of who had really murdered Sadie Wadford, but he vowed to make sure justice was done. Sometimes money and position meant crimes got swept under the rug, but Stone refused to let that happen this time.

A few minutes later he heard the sound of someone coming up the trail, the muffled noise of boots moving through the snow, the labored breathing of a man no longer in peak physical condition.

"Morning," Stone greeted as Camden climbed into view.

The sheriff nodded. "Preacher." He leaned forward for a moment, hands on his knees, catching his breath.

"Sounds like maybe you need less fried food and more exercise."

Camden straightened up and cut right to the chase. "What I need is for you to stop playing games and give me this proof you have that Nugent didn't kill Sadie."

"Sure thing," Stone said. "It's getting cold up here and I'm ready for a big plate of bacon and home fries. But before breakfast comes justice, right?" He pulled out his cell phone. "I've got a video you need to watch."

Camden gave Stone a squinty-eyed look that seemed to say, *What the hell are you up to, preacher?* Then he looked down at the screen as Stone started the video.

The video of the man in the wolf mask raping Sadie Wadford.

The video of the man in the wolf mask chasing her through the swamp.

The video of the man in the wolf mask cutting her throat.

The video of the wolf mask being removed to reveal the killer.

The video of Sheriff Camden.

The sheriff reached for his Glock but it was a waste of time. Stone already had the Smith & Wesson .44 Magnum leveled at him.

"Don't do it," Stone warned.

Camden moved his hand away from his sidearm. "So what now?" he growled.

"So now you tell me why you did it."

"Money," Camden replied. "Why else? That shit goes for a pretty penny to the right buyer and being sheriff of Garrison County ain't exactly making me rich."

"Don't worry, you're not going to be the sheriff much longer." Stone dropped the phone back into his pocket. "And I think it was about more than just the money. You looked like you were enjoying yourself, you sick son of a bitch."

"Yeah?" Camden stuck out his chin in a gesture of

defiance. "And what if I did? Who the hell are you to judge me?"

"I'm not going to judge you," Stone said. "God is. Take off your clothes."

"What? I'm not stripping for you, asshole!"

"Take them off or I'll shoot you in the gut and leave you here to die. At least the other way, you have a chance."

"What other way? What kind of chance?"

"I'm going to leave you up here, naked, with a blizzard coming in soon. If God chooses to let you live, then so be it." He thumbed back the .44's hammer, the ratcheting of metal ominously loud in the cold stillness of the woods. "Or I can blow a hole in your belly right now. Your choice."

"You bastard," Camden hissed. But he started stripping.

Stone watched impassively as the sheriff removed his clothes. He made him toss his Glock into the trees in one direction and his cellphone in the other direction. Both vanished into snowdrifts. By the time Camden got down to his boxers, he was shivering so hard that his bones threatened to rattle right out of his goosebumped skin.

"Satisfied?" the sheriff said, teeth chattering like castanets.

"Negative," Stone replied. "You're going to face God as naked as the day you were born."

Camden snarled an obscenity, shucked off his boxers, and said, "I think you just want to see my pecker."

"It's not about seeing your dick," Stone said. "It's about making sure nothing's in the way of the coywolves tearing it off when they come calling."

"Not gonna happen, preacher. I'm walking off this damn mountain and when I do, you're a dead man."

"Thought you might say something like that," Stone said, and shot him in the kneecaps.

The snow was coming down harder now, but not nearly enough to muffle the thunderous roar of the .44 Magnum. The sheriff's knees exploded like hammered ice. He fell to the ground, screaming as blood spurted from the broken mess of bone and gristle that had been his joints.

Stone lowered the revolver. "Unless God feels like wasting a miracle on a kid-killing piece of shit like you, you're not going to be walking anywhere."

He holstered the revolver, kicked Camden's clothes over the edge of the waterfall, and then headed back down the mountain, leaving the naked, crippled, screaming, scumbag sheriff writhing in the red-splattered snow. With the storm coming on strong, the wind had picked up and the scent of blood would be carried along on the icy currents. Even from a mile or more away, the hungry coy-wolves would smell the blood and be summoned to a fresh feast.

If Camden even lived that long.

Picking his way down the trail through the steadily-accumulating snow, Stone didn't much care whether the bastard froze to death or got his throat ripped out by wild fangs.

Just as long as he died and went to hell.

Sadie—and all those other girls—deserved justice.

Stone was halfway down the mountain before he could no longer hear the sheriff's screams.

―――――

Back at the church, Stone sat in his office with a hot cup of coffee and stared out the window at the snow coming down. It was really pounding now, the world turning white as a classic Nor'easter blizzard swept into town. At least another three inches had fallen since he left Camden on top of Whisper Falls. Give it another hour or two and the body would be buried until spring.

Max laid at his feet. A Bible laid on the desk, the Smith & Wesson Stealth Hunter Performance .44 Magnum lying beside it. Out of these three things, only one of them was sacred, but they all brought him comfort.

He knew the scriptures well. Knew the commandment not to kill. But he felt no remorse at taking the sheriff's life. Maybe he should…but he didn't. The guilt might come later, when he took the time to pray about it, to ask for God's understanding. And if not understanding, then forgiveness. Maybe then God would strike his conscience. But right now, he felt like what was done, was done.

He reached down, ruffled the dog's ears, and said, "It's finished, Max. All that's left now is learning how to live with it."

EPILOGUE

THE CHRISTMAS EVE blizzard dumped nearly three feet of snow on the region before swirling north into Canada. It was five months later before hikers found Camden's frozen remains. Wasn't much of him left; predators had stripped his carcass to the bone.

By then, the buzz over the sheriff's disappearance had abated. He'd been linked to the child rape-murder ring that was discovered when the Feds raided the survivalist compound, so nobody in town much cared what had happened to him. Deputy Valentine currently filled the void until the governor got around to appointing a new placeholder sheriff.

Stone made some calls to ensure no crimes landed on his doorstep. The FBI took full credit for busting the survivalists and their official report indicated the survivalists had turned on each other, resulting in a deadly shootout that left no survivors.

The shooting of Blackbeard—he never did learn the guy's real name—had been ruled self-defense, a justifiable homicide. Holly's handler in the U.S. Marshals assured her that they did not consider her cover blown, so she could stay in Whisper Falls.

Stone still sometimes struggled with what he had done. Long talks with Max and God—and not in that particular order—helped, but he also knew that he would kill a dozen pedophilic butchers again and again if that's what it took to keep Holly and Lizzy in his life.

Once news of the horrific atrocities the survivalists had committed out there in the swamp made the headlines, Stone confronted Mason Xavier. The businessman and rumored crime boss of Garrison County emphatically denied any knowledge of what his enforcers had been involved with.

"They are on my payroll to provide security when called upon," Xavier had said. "I have never even set foot on their compound. What they do—or rather, did—on their own time was not my concern."

"You've got a real talent for hiring scumbags," Stone had replied.

"Perhaps. But poor business decisions do not make me an accomplice to the crimes of my employees."

"It does if you knew about those crimes."

"Which I did not."

Stone had no proof of Xavier's involvement—the businessman had not appeared on any of the videos he had seen—so there was no justification to deep-six him.

Not yet, anyway.

Stone threw on a flannel shirt and went out onto his deck. It might be May and most of the snow gone, especially in the valleys, but the morning air was still cool. He still had some repair work to be done on the house from the autofire assault it had suffered back in December, but it had been fixed up enough for him to live in again, thank God. Sleeping on the couch in his office had gotten real old, real fast.

He settled down in one of the chairs, smiling as Max flopped down beside him with an overly dramatic sigh that seemed to say, *What are we doing out here when it's nice and warm inside?*

He picked up his cell phone and made a call he'd been thinking about for quite some time.

It took nearly fifteen minutes and vetting by three different people before the man he wanted to talk to came on the line.

"Lucas Stone. I'll be damned. Great to hear from you. How's life on the other side?"

"Different, sir, but good."

"I'd love to have a beer sometime and hear all about it, but today is not that day. I hate to cut you short, Luke, but I've got a teleconference with the Russian Prime Minister in five minutes, so why don't we save the catching up for another time and you just get right down to telling me what you need."

"No problem." Stone spelled it out for him.

"You sure that's what you want to do? I thought you were looking to walk away from that sort of thing."

"Just trying to take care of my little corner of the world."

"Somebody's gotta do it, right?" The man chuckled. "That was always your motto."

"Can you make it happen?"

"Of course I can. I'll make the call as soon as I'm done with Russia." The man chuckled again. "A gun in one hand, a Bible in the other. Isn't that an oxymoron or something?"

"The Lord works in mysterious ways."

"You can say that again." The man paused, then said, "Good hearing from you, Luke. Thanks for everything you did for us back in the day. You're a good man with a good heart. Keep the faith."

"Always."

He hung up, then sat and watched the world go by as he waited for his phone to ring. The flannel warded off the morning chill and the sun creeping over the tree-lined ridge to the east felt good on his face.

When his phone rang forty-five minutes later, he picked it up and said, "Hello."

"Is this Lucas Stone?"

"It is."

"This is the governor."

"Thought you might be calling."

"Well, it's not often that the President of the United States gives me a ring and strongly encourages me to appoint you to the vacant sheriff position in Garrison County."

Stone didn't say anything. He thought, *Do I really want to do this?*

"Luke, are you still there?" the governor asked.

"I'm here."

"So do you want the job? It would just be until the next election, which is eighteen months away."

Somebody's gotta do it.

"Yeah, sure. I'll take it."

"Great, glad to hear it. I'll have my office make all the official notifications. Congratulations, Mr. Stone, you're the new sheriff of Garrison County."

"Thanks. I appreciate it."

Stone set down the phone. It was done. No turning back now.

He was a man of faith and a man of the law. But he was also a man who believed in justice. And sometimes justice could only be found outside the rigid parameters of righteousness and legalities. Sometimes justice came from the shadows, not the light.

Preacher. Sheriff. Vigilante.

He wasn't sure how he was going to make it all work, but he knew one thing for certain.

He damn sure was going to try.

A LOOK AT BOOK TWO:
THE BAD SAMARITAN

Things get hot in Whisper Falls when a string of arsons sets the town on edge. When the latest fire causes the death of a beloved citizen and all signs point to the husband, Garrison County becomes a powder keg ready to blow. Lucas Stone, a former black ops specialist who is now the sheriff, knows that he needs to get to the bottom of things before his quiet town is filled with nothing but flames and death.

Then a local girl is burned alive and all hell breaks loose. Who is behind the killing? Why did they target an innocent kid? When another girl is abducted, the countdown is on to save her life before she, too, meets a horrific, fiery end.

Stone will move heaven and earth to find her. Because when law and order go up in smoke, the only thing that remains is primal justice.

AVAILABLE FEBRUARY 2023

ABOUT THE AUTHOR

Mark Allen was raised by an ancient clan of ruthless ninjas and now that he has revealed this dark secret, he will most likely be dead by tomorrow for breaking the sacred oath of silence. The ninjas take this stuff very seriously.

When not practicing his shuriken-throwing techniques or browsing flea markets for a new katana, Mark writes action fiction. He prefers his pose to pack a punch, likes his heroes to sport twin Micro-Uzis a la Chuck Norris in Invasion USA, and firmly believes there is no such thing as too many headshots in a novel.

He started writing "guns 'n' guts" (his term for the action genre) at the not-so-tender age of 16 and soon won his first regional short story contest. His debut action novel, The Assassin's Prayer, was optioned by Showtime for a direct-to-cable movie. When that didn't pan out, he published the book on Amazon to great success, moving over 10,000 copies in its first year, thanks to its visceral combination of raw, redemptive drama mixed with unflinching violence.

Now, as part of the Wolfpack team, Mark Allen looks forward to bringing his bloody brand of gun-slinging, bullet-blasting mayhem to the action-reading masses.

Mark currently resides in the Adirondack Mountains of upstate New York with a wife who doubts his ninja skills because he's always slicing his fingers while chopping veggies, two daughters who refuse to take tae kwon do, let alone ninjitsu, and enough firepower to ensure that he is never bothered by door-to-door salesmen.

Made in the USA
Las Vegas, NV
03 September 2023

77005601R00152